TEA IS FOR TOXIN

A HAUNTED TEAROOM COZY MYSTERY

KAREN SUE WALKER

LARAGRAY PRESS

∽

For more information about me and all my books or to contact me, visit http://karensuewalker.com.

ACKNOWLEDGEMENTS

My gorgeous cover was designed by Mariah Sinclair, aka the Cozy Queen. Find her at https://www.thecovervault.com or on Facebook.

My copy editor is Alyssa Linn Palmer. Thank you for your expertise and swift turnaround!

Finally, to my wonderful readers. You give me inspiration, ideas, moral support, and encouragement (and find the most persistent of typos!). You are what makes all the hard work worthwhile.

CHAPTER 1

*S*erenity Cove pretended to be the sort of place where nothing bad ever happened. The beautiful, secluded seaside town in northern California, population 964, held its share of secrets. I'd learned that some people will do anything to keep the truth from coming out.

My name is April May, and last month, on a whim, I bought a huge Victorian house and decided to open a tearoom on the first floor. Perhaps it was my version of a mid-life crisis as I approached the big five-oh, but I liked to think of it as a chance to start over and have the life I really wanted.

The tearoom had come with a few surprises—a Bengal cat named Whisk in the attic, the ghost of a French chef in the kitchen, and an antique desk with hidden drawers full of diamond, emerald, and ruby jewelry. The jewels, as it turned out, legally belonged to me. No living relatives of the woman who'd once owned them could be found.

With just ten days to prepare for SereniTea's grand opening, my to-do list stretched a mile long. I spent most of my time in my spacious, shiny-white kitchen perfecting recipes, with my ghost-chef watching over my shoulder. Chef Emile Toussaint entertained and vexed me in equal measures. He seemed determined to make a passable chef out of me by alternately praising and insulting my efforts.

He observed me preparing choux pastry on the stove. "Lower the flame. Do you want to burn the butter?"

"Chill out," I said, getting a confused look from the chef in return. "I've got it under control." I took the pot off the stove just as the doorbell rang.

Irritation crept up my spine, since it probably meant a solicitor. Friends came through the back door. I stepped through the tearoom, which took up the entire first floor except for the kitchen and one former bedroom. My sneakers gave a little squeak as I stepped on the diamond-shaped blue and cream tiles and past flowered tablecloths and sparkling chandeliers.

I opened the front door to greet the visitor, who pushed past me. The round-faced, frizzy-haired woman wore a bright orange T-shirt with a logo emblazoned across her chest. It read, "Fiends of the Library." I did a double take. Yep. It said fiends.

"We're not open yet," I explained, annoyed by her pushiness. If she'd given me a moment, I would have invited her in. If she'd asked nicely, I might have even offered her a cup of tea. I even had freshly baked palmiers, delicious French pastries, cooling on a rack in the kitchen. She had no idea what her rudeness had cost her.

"Are you April May?"

"Yes, but my grand opening isn't until a week from Saturday. Would you like to make a reservation for later in June?" I pasted on a friendly smile. "We're also available for special events."

"I'm soliciting donations for the Friends of the Library," she said.

I squinted at her shirt. "But it says—"

"I know what it says," she snapped. "We don't have the budget to redo the shirts right now. There are more important priorities."

"I didn't even know we had a library." Serenity Cove didn't boast a lot of amenities, so you'd think I'd have noticed a library, especially since I loved to read.

She sighed. "They closed it several years ago during the budget crisis. We're raising funds to qualify for a matching grant so we can reopen it."

Turning my grand opening into a fundraiser sounded like a great idea, and reopening the library seemed to be a worthy cause. Besides, it might help me win over more of the locals.

Another woman paced on the front lawn in a matching orange shirt, along with a floppy hat and sunglasses. Why was the mayor's secretary in disguise?

I stepped out onto the porch. "Is that you, Pauline?"

Her mouth dropped open, and she spun on her heel, hurrying down the street. The other woman ran after her, calling out, "Come back, Pauline. I'm sure she won't tell the mayor."

MY ONE EMPLOYEE, Jennifer Skillings, had rented a room from me when her father forced her to choose between working for me or living at home. Barely an adult, she had the enthusiasm of a teenager and the sense of responsibility of someone much older.

On this morning, Jennifer wore her dirty-blonde hair in two pigtails. She made a mean cappuccino, which meant friends often stopped by for their morning coffee and a visit.

Chef Emile stirred an invisible pot on the stove, seemingly engrossed in whatever dish he prepared. Despite his feigned inattention, he listened to every word said in his presence.

The first friend to stop by was Kyla Bradley, a reporter for the local TV station. Dark haired and elegant, she always appeared ready for her closeup. I handed her a freshly-baked cream puff, which she accepted gratefully.

She raised her voice to be heard over the hissing espresso machine. "How are the plans for your grand opening proceeding?" she asked, raising one perfectly groomed eyebrow.

"I'm thinking about turning it into a fundraiser for the library," I said. "You were in town when they closed it, weren't you?"

"I did a number of stories on it," she said. "Not that it did any good. The county had a funding crisis, and barely enough in the budget for essential services. The previous mayor had promised to reopen it, but Mayor Gasden has other ideas."

Jennifer handed Kyla the first coffee drink. She took a sip, then daintily dabbed her red lips on a napkin.

"What kind of ideas?" I asked Kyla.

We were interrupted by a knock at the back door. Irma, the owner of the Mermaid Café, entered wearing an oversized man's trench coat. She wore huge, red-framed glasses and styled her gray hair in short spikes. She made up for her diminutive size with her no-nonsense attitude and brusque demeanor, which I found endearing.

"Cream puffs?" Irma asked, in a thinly veiled hint.

I placed a cream puff on a plate and set in front of her usual spot at the kitchen island. Irma threw her coat over one stool and perched on another. Jennifer continued frothing milk while I repeated my idea for the grand opening.

"A fundraiser to reopen the library?" Irma asked, eyeing the treat eagerly. "I think it's a smashing idea. We've been without a library for far too long. I heard the mayor wants to turn it into a food court."

I grimaced at the thought. "We need a theme, or better yet, a celebrity if we want to raise a lot of money. And I don't have much time to put it together."

Kyla gave me a thoughtful look. "There are a few semi-famous people who used to live here. I learned quite a bit about them during my research." Everyone knew about the tell-all book she planned to publish, which made many of the residents of Serenity Cove uneasy. No one wanted their secrets exposed.

"Who, that soap opera star?" Irma asked. "Daniela Dumont is a washed-up has-been." She turned to me. "I bet you can hire her cheap."

Kyla gave Irma a smirk. "I'll see if I can touch base and find someone to make an appearance at your grand opening."

"What about you?" I asked Kyla. "You're a local celebrity."

Irma and Jennifer agreed, though Kyla brushed off our comment.

"You'd sell more tickets with a real celebrity," Kyla said. "And the more tickets you sell, the more money for the library. But I'd be happy to emcee if you can't find anyone."

"I know," Irma blurted out. "Why don't you use the jewelry to help raise some dough?"

"A raffle for a diamond necklace?" I hoped that wasn't what she meant.

"Sacre bleu!" Emile cried out, startling me. Apparently, he didn't like the idea of me selling off Norma's jewelry. I hoped the others hadn't noticed me jump.

Irma chortled. "Heck no! I was thinking you could display them."

"Oh, of course." It would make more sense to sell one of the pieces and donate the money, but I wouldn't say that out loud in front of the chef. The jewels had belonged to Norma, the woman who'd lived in the house decades earlier and who'd hired Emile when she'd turned the first floor into a French restaurant. Chef had been in love with Norma, although he'd never told her.

"That's a great idea," Kyla said. "I bet lots of people would love to see them, out of curiosity if nothing else."

"You mean display them like a museum?" I'd heard worse ideas. "There are only five necklaces, plus a few earrings and bracelets. Not much to show off."

Jennifer handed me a latte. "And that gorgeous brooch."

"Ugh," Irma said. "That thing is hideous. If you're going to make a diamond-encrusted bug, why not a butterfly or a ladybug? What's it supposed to be, anyway?"

"It's a beetle," Jennifer said with a scowl. "At least, I think that's what it is. Insect brooches were very popular back in the forties, and I think it's delightful."

"Even with the scary brooch, it's not much of a display," I said. "Do you think anyone would want to come and see a few pieces of jewelry?"

"Maybe Jennifer could loan you some of her vintage dresses," Kyla suggested. "Set up some mannequins around the room, and sort of recreate the past."

"I love that idea." Jennifer handed Irma her drink. "But I don't have any nice dresses from that era. Most of my mid-century outfits are more casual."

"Too bad you didn't keep the dresses Norma gave you back then," I said to Irma. She'd been a hostess at Norma's restaurant when she was just a teenager, and Norma had given Irma many of her couture and designer dresses once she'd tired of them.

Irma raised her eyebrows but said nothing.

"Or did you?" Fundraiser or not, I wanted to see those dresses.

"Perhaps," Irma said. "There might be two or three that I kept."

CHAPTER 2

*a*s I hummed a happy tune, I pulled a muffin tin full of mini quiche Lorraines from the oven and transferred them to a rack to cool.

"What do you think? Do they meet your approval?"

The ghost of Emile Toussaint looked up from his writing. "They'll do. Although, it's beyond me why you don't make a traditional quiche. Perhaps you are not aware one can slice a quiche into individual servings."

I held up a mini-quiche and waved it in front of him. "But these are cute."

His nose went up in the air and he huffed, "Cute? Since when does cute have a place in modern cuisine?"

Chef Emile had been dead since the early 1960s, so I felt sure I knew more about modern cuisine than he did even if he had written *Modern French Cooking*, and its two sequels. Ever since he turned up in my kitchen, he'd been full of advice, whether I wanted it or not. When I first saw him, I'd thought I'd hallucinated, but I finally came to terms with the fact that he was an actual ghost who'd taken up residence in my kitchen.

I hadn't told anyone else about him, because I didn't want them to think I had gone cuckoo. As far as I knew, I was the only one privileged to see him. If he had unfinished business on the mortal plane, he hadn't shared it with me.

Three sharp raps on the back door meant that Irma had stopped back by to mooch snacks. She always had some excuse for showing up when she knew I'd be baking. I didn't mind. In spite of her irascible nature, she'd become a friend, and I needed allies in Serenity Cove. The town didn't exactly welcome newcomers with open arms, but they seemed to have grudgingly accepted that I was here to stay.

"Quiche again?" she asked as she pulled a stool up to the kitchen island that served as workspace and kitchen table.

"Ham and leek mini ones this time. I tried one of Chef's variations." I put a warm quiche on a plate and set it in front of her. "If you'd like to give me your opinion."

"I suppose I could do that for you." She gobbled it down in two bites and I handed her a napkin to wipe the crumbs from her face. Her mouth full, she nodded and gave me a thumbs up.

"I'm glad at least someone approves." I gave Chef Emile a pointed glare, but he ignored me.

"Someone doesn't? Who could say anything bad about mini quiches?"

"It's just that Chef is so traditional." I corrected myself. "I mean his recipes are."

That caught Emile's attention. "Now there is something wrong with tradition?" he sniffed.

Irma shook her head. "I'm starting to worry about you. You talk about him as if he's alive--like you've been talking to him."

I laughed nervously. "That's impossible."

"Not necessarily. I think I've figured it out. I'm not sure why you're keeping it a secret. I'd understand, you know."

"Understand what?" She couldn't possibly know. Could she?

She narrowed her eyes. "You've found a journal of his, haven't you? That's how you know he called me his 'petite carotte.' What else did he say about me? Can I see it?"

Chef Emile chuckled. "Ah, I can picture her now, flitting around the kitchen, sneaking carrots, and distracting my sous chef with her flirtatious antics."

I smiled at his description of young Irma. If I told her there was a journal, it would protect my secret. But I didn't want to lie, and besides, I had nothing to show her. "There's no journal."

"Fine. Don't tell me." She stood and put her plate in the sink. "I've got to get going."

"Are you mad?" I asked as she walked toward the door. She didn't answer.

"Yep," I said to Chef as the door slammed. "She's mad."

I glanced at the clock—nearly five p.m. "I'm going to feed Whisk before he thinks I've completely forgotten about him." Chef Emile didn't look up from his writing. I'd asked him if he was putting together another cookbook to go along with the three that had been published in the early sixties, but he shook his head. He didn't seem to want me to know what he was working on.

I took the cat's bowl up two flights of stairs to the attic. Whisk came with the house, and I didn't like to think what he'd survived on for the few weeks the house had stood uninhabited. He'd made it clear to me I wasn't to close the window that allowed him to come and go as he pleased. His favorite chair sat empty, so I called his name and put the bowl on the floor.

I hadn't seen him in two days, which wasn't unusual, but I felt a tug of worry about the little guy, so I went looking for him.

I'd bought the house with all its contents, including an attic full of furniture and boxes. I'd cleared a path between the boxes and furniture, but the space was still half full.

"Whisk?" I called again, making my way toward the back of the attic. Instead of the cat, I found a puddle. That couldn't be good. They'd done a roof inspection when I'd bought the house, and I hoped they hadn't missed something. Looked like another job for the local handyman, Mark Nazari.

I moved some of the furniture and boxes away from the leak. I'd been slowly going through the boxes, finding old photos and mementos, but little of any value. I peered into one and found a small leopard curled up inside. That's what Whisk looked like to me, though after an internet search, I identified him as a Bengal cat.

"Hey, Whisk. What are you doing in there?"

The cat looked up and said "Yowrr," which I took to mean, "Go away, don't bother me."

"Okay, I just wanted to let you know I brought your food." I took a closer look. The cat sat on a pile of documents of some sort, but when I reached for them, Whisk hissed at me. That wasn't the first time he'd told me in cat language to back off.

"Fine," I said, not wanting to admit a cat had hurt my feelings.

MONDAY MORNING, I opened my eyes and groaned. I knew that getting older beat the alternative, but I didn't feel prepared to be a fifty-year-old woman. Shouldn't I be wiser?

Crawling out of bed, I slid into my slippers and shuffled to the parlor window, looking out at the fog that obscured my ocean view. If one more person said "May gray" to me, I might slug them.

A moment later, the sun emerged, a beam of light breaking through the haze. I took it as a sign. A brighter future waited for me. Why not? There'd been a lot of ups and downs in my first fifty years of life. It was time for some smooth sailing.

Besides, my new friends were throwing me a birthday party.

I dressed and hurried downstairs. Jennifer waited for me in the kitchen with a freshly brewed cappuccino.

"You spoil me." I grinned and pulled a stool up to the island. Having Jennifer renting a room from me was like having a resident barista.

"It's your birthday." She practically bounced around the kitchen, popping bread into the toaster and squeezing fresh orange juice. "I'm sorry I can't cook."

"No sorrys, remember?" I gently scolded her, though I doubted I'd ever break her of the habit. She apologized for everything, whether it was her fault or not.

"Sorry." She put her hand in front of her mouth. "Oops!"

I laughed. "We have the whole morning free, and I'm not going to work on my birthday. The to-do list is going to have to wait until tomorrow." It was a really long list. "What should we do?"

"I have an idea." Her voice sounded tentative, as if she were up to something.

I hesitated. "Yes?"

"Can I give you a makeover?" Her smile tightened as she waited for my reaction.

I'd managed to go my entire life without a makeover and wondered what I might be getting myself into. "Will it be painful?"

"No, of course not!" She must have taken my response as acceptance, because she began explaining what she planned for the morning.

She seemed so happy that I didn't have the heart to say no, even though the idea filled me with apprehension.

"You're not going to cut all my hair off, are you?" When she promised no scissors would be involved, I gave into the inevitable and managed to pretend mild enthusiasm. "Sure, why not."

Jennifer raised her eyebrows at the sound of the doorbell. "Expecting someone?"

"Must be Mark." I headed for the front door, passing tables and chairs already set up for the tearoom opening. I greeted Mark Nazari, my handyman with a smile. "Come in."

Every woman should have a hot handyman, and Mark, dark-haired and handsome, fit the bill. He wore his sleeves rolled up as if to give me a peek at his muscular arms. Perhaps when the weather warmed, he would wear a tight T-shirt. A girl could hope.

"Good morning, April." He held something behind his back which he produced with a flourish, handing me a bouquet of colorful spring flowers. "Happy birthday."

"Thank you." I gave him a spontaneous hug. I might have held onto him a few seconds more than necessary, but he didn't object. "Join us in the kitchen, and Jennifer will make you a cappuccino."

"Thanks," he said, "but I think I'll get to work. Can you show me where the water's getting in?"

He followed me up two flights of stairs into the attic. "Watch your step up here," he warned. "Make sure you step on the crossbeams. It looks like some of the floorboards have rotted, probably from the moisture."

"Uh-huh," I said, wondering how much this would cost me.

"Did you hear what I said?" he repeated. "Watch your step."

"Got it." I showed him where I'd spotted the leak then

came downstairs, rejoining Jennifer in the kitchen. Three quick raps on the door meant Irma had arrived. She entered wearing a leather jacket and fedora, and Jennifer got up to make her favorite caramel latte.

"Happy birthday." Irma pulled up a stool and pointed at the half muffin still on my plate. "Are you going to finish that?"

I pushed the plate toward her. "No time for breakfast this morning?"

She sighed dramatically and took a bite of muffin. "Do you know how much work is involved in planning a birthday party?"

Never having planned one, I merely shrugged.

Irma chewed her muffin and scowled. "Do you know how hard it is to plan a menu when the birthday girl is such a picky eater?"

"Me? A picky eater?" That seemed an overstatement. "Just because I don't want to burn off my tongue? I told you to just let me know what dishes were spicy and I'd avoid them."

"Or have bell peppers or olives." Irma sulked as she finished my muffin, and I guessed she felt under-appreciated.

Maybe I needed to show more gratitude. "You're right," I said. "I'm such a picky eater, and it must have been so much work to come up with a menu avoiding of all the foods I won't eat."

She narrowed her eyes suspiciously, but a small smile appeared, letting me know she felt appeased. "That's right. Just because it's a buffet doesn't mean there can be a hodge-podge of foods with absolutely no rhyme or reason."

"Of course not." Then, to change the subject, I added, "Jennifer's giving me a makeover."

Irma's expression morphed into a grin. "It's about time. Are you going to do something with that mousy hair?"

I frowned. "Aren't people supposed to be nice to you on your birthday?"

Irma snickered, which annoyed me even more. "You have lovely hair." She took off her hat and ruffled her short, gray hair. "At least yours isn't thinning like mine. Still, give it time."

I shook my head. With a friend like Irma, I never had to worry about getting too big of an ego.

CHAPTER 3

*J*ennifer plopped me on a folding chair in the upstairs master bathroom and wrapped a towel around my neck. Bottles, jars, and other items took up every available horizontal surface, and a curling iron rested precariously on the edge of the sink.

She smeared a fragrant substance onto my face and told me not to smile while it dried. I was about to tell her that smiling was the furthest thing from my mind when she shushed me.

"And no talking," she added. "This will do wonders for your complexion."

She hummed while brushing my hair, and I closed my eyes, my thoughts drifting to my mother. Loving, kind, and unpredictable, she had lived life on a rollercoaster and took me along for the ride. On some days, she'd brushed and braided my hair and on others, failed to notice that I had no clean clothes to wear.

Remember the good parts. It had become my mantra.

An hour later, after hair, makeup, and wardrobe, Jennifer

took two steps back and held her arms out. "You look amazing."

I thought that might be overstating it, but when I glanced in the mirror, I liked what I saw. "I wish I had a pair of heels to wear with this dress."

She held up a pair of strappy sandals, and I grabbed her in a hug.

"What are you wearing?" I loved seeing Jennifer's parade of quirky outfits, usually vintage or reproductions.

"I got a new poodle skirt," she said. "A pink one."

"Will you be wearing your saddle shoes?" I felt a little envious, since I normally preferred wearing flats.

"Of course! Saddle shoes, bobby socks and a ponytail."

Between my heels clomping on the wood hallway and Jennifer's happy chattering, we made enough noise for Mark to emerge from the attic. He stood in the open doorway and stared. I checked to make sure I didn't have my dress tucked into my panties, but everything seemed to be in order.

"What?" I asked.

"You look beautiful."

I may have stopped breathing for just a moment, because I felt lightheaded and grabbed for the banister. I remembered my manners, and said, "Thank you."

He gave me a grin before slipping back into the attic.

Jennifer loaned me a jacket from her collection of vintage clothing to keep me warm on the walk to Irma's restaurant and we headed out. As we strolled along the beach, we talked about who we'd likely see at my party.

I hadn't been in town long, so having Jennifer, Irma, and Freddie as friends seemed good enough to me. "I'd be happy if it's just the four of us." I knew I couldn't be that lucky.

"Pauline is coming," she said. "I invited the mayor just to be polite, but I doubt she'll show. Oh, and Kyla, of course."

"Great." I considered Kyla a friend, though I hadn't had a

17

chance to get to know her well. "I suppose everyone will want to ask her about the novel she's writing."

"That's all anyone can talk about," Jennifer said. "Does everyone in this town have secrets they want to hide?"

"Not me. What about you?"

She looked surprised by my question. "Me? What could I be hiding? I'm barely old enough to drink."

"You made it," Irma called out from behind the bar the moment we walked in the door. "Hey, you look good."

I blinked as my eyes became accustomed to the dim interior of the Mermaid Cafe. Undulating aqua lights gave the restaurant an underwater feel, and as usual, transported me to another world. I headed for the long, acrylic bar, lit from within and filled with sand and shells. A few people sat at the bar, but the booths and tables were empty.

"Where are all your customers?" I asked.

"Didn't you see the sign outside?" When I didn't respond, she explained that it would be a private party until seven, at which time, she'd open for dinner.

Irma picked up a cocktail shaker and gave it a jiggle. "Lemon drop?" She poured the liquor into two martini glasses, handing one to me and one to Jennifer.

I took a sip, closing my eyes to savor the sweet and sour concoction. "Delicious."

Jennifer picked up her drink. "To April." She clinked her glass against mine. "Happy birthday."

Irma pulled a beer from underneath the bar and tapped the bottle against my martini glass. "Cheers. Remember, only the good die young, so you'd better start being bad." She gave me a wink. "I'd start with the handyman, if I were you."

"Irma!" I pretended to be shocked by her suggestion. At

that moment, the door opened, and a female figure appeared, silhouetted in the bright outdoor light.

The woman took a step inside and swept her coat from her shoulders in a gesture I recognized. "Hi, Kyla."

"April, there you are." She approached me and gave me air kisses. Handing me a birthday card, she told me she'd included a gift certificate for the finest spa in the nearby town of Somerville. "When I say the finest, I mean the only one, of course."

"At least they have one. Thanks so much." I gave her a hug. "I can't wait to try it out." When I moved to Serenity Cove, I hadn't been aware of the limited services and shopping. Most of the time I didn't mind, but sometimes I wished I didn't have to drive twenty minutes just to go to the hardware store or get a pedicure. Maybe I should have opened a combination hardware store and nail salon instead of a tearoom. It might have been a big hit.

Checking out the room, I pointed out three men at the other end of the bar. "Who are they?" I asked Irma.

"That's my accountant," Irma said. "He's around your age. I told him to bring some friends in case he wasn't your type."

"Are you serious?" I hoped the ground would open up and swallow me, but since that wasn't likely to happen, I pasted on a smile and gave them a little wave.

"What's wrong with him?" Irma groused. "Not your type?"

"It was very thoughtful of you, and I'm sure they're very nice men, but I'd rather enjoy my friends without trying to make small talk with people I barely know."

"Have it your way." She left to take the men's drink orders.

Kyla kept her eye on the door, tensing every time it opened and relaxing when she appeared to recognize each new arrival. When Jennifer's father arrived, it was my turn to tense. He stood just inside the door looking for someone—his daughter, I guessed.

"Dad?" Jennifer said when she noticed him. "What are you doing here?"

"Is that any way to greet your father?" He gave me a friendly smile and his daughter a hug. "Happy birthday, April. Jennifer tells me you like exotic teas." He handed me a small gift bag. "You might not have tried this one."

I pulled a container of Pink Chai loose tea from the bag. "Thank you. That's very thoughtful."

"It has cardamom and beetroot. The beetroot gives it the pink color." He paused as if not sure what to say next or perhaps how to say it. "You've been so good to my daughter, and I just wanted to thank you. And to apologize for before, when I…"

"No apology necessary." Sure, he'd pretty much accused me of being a murderer, but then, nearly everyone else in town had thought I was guilty when a body had been found in my home. Glancing at Jennifer, my heart warmed seeing how happy she looked. She and her father had been estranged for over a month, and I knew how hard it had been on her. After all, he was her only family.

While they caught up, it seemed like a good opportunity to get to know Kyla better. I tapped her on her shoulder, and she jumped. She'd turned her cocktail napkin into a twisted clump of paper.

I lowered my voice. "I've heard not everyone is happy about the novel you're writing."

Her mouth twisted into a grimace. "That's an understatement. Some people would do almost anything to make sure I didn't publish it. I've uncovered plenty of secrets. There was even a murder in this town, though you won't find it in any of the newspapers from the time." She glanced over her shoulder. "Can we talk later?"

A man not much taller than me wearing a huge cowboy hat and a bushy mustache approached her. Kyla's eyes narrowed, but a smile played on her lips. Did she know this man?

Freddie arrived, so I went to greet her by the door. Dr. Fredeline Severs was the only doctor in town and the coroner for our sparsely populated county. Her upbeat personality would liven up the party. She wore a form-fitted mini dress that showed off her glowing, brown skin. She'd styled her hair in tight, bouncy curls.

She spotted me and headed our way. "You look great."

I grinned. "All thanks to Jennifer's fairy magic. I turn back into a pumpkin at midnight, unlike you. You look amazing."

"Hey, Doc," Irma said. "Go get some food before all the good stuff's gone. You too, April."

Freddie and I headed past two couples dancing to the beat of the music.

"Who are they?" I asked, wondering why Irma had invited strangers to my party.

"That's Irma's dentist and his wife. I think the other couple are friends of theirs."

"So, Irma invited her accountant *and* her dentist to my party?" I laughed. "At least it makes it look like I'm more popular than I am."

The music got louder, and before I could grab a plate, one of the accountant's friends pulled me out onto the dance floor. He leaned close to talk, yelling in my ear, "I hear it's your birthday." His breath smelled of beer.

Giving him a polite nod, I hid my annoyance at his intruding on my pleasant evening. I shuffled my feet in a way that hopefully resembled dancing while deciding how soon I could make my escape.

"Let me guess." He smirked. "Twenty-nine."

Before I could correct him, he grabbed my hand,

attempting to lead me in an awkward move and gave me a twirl. My hand slipped from his, and I spun right into the chest of a tall and very handsome stranger, who took me into his arms as if the whole maneuver had been planned.

"Well, hello there," he said, with an amused smile. "Care to dance?"

"Sorry about that." Although, at that moment, I didn't feel the least bit sorry.

He had light brown hair, slightly thinning but perfectly styled, and smile lines next to his eyes.

I swayed in his arms, breathing in the soft, herbal scent of his cologne. "I'm April."

"Ah, the birthday girl. You're new in town, aren't you?"

"Yes. Let me guess. You're Irma's financial planner," I half joked.

His amber eyes twinkled with curiosity. "No.... I'm in town on business before jetting off to Tuscany for a few weeks." He guided me effortlessly around the dance floor, as if I were light as a feather. "My name is Sebastian. Sebastian Bernini."

"What sort of business?" He seemed charming, if a bit pompous. Who called getting on a plane "jetting?" Unless he had his own private jet.

"My childhood home requires some renovations before it can be leased again. I'm here to check on the progress. Although, I may stay a bit longer than planned. It seems as though the scenery has improved since I left town."

CHAPTER 4

*D*id Sebastian mean what I think he meant? It had been so long since anyone had flirted with me, I didn't know how to act. I just gave him a grin that probably made me look demented.

He glanced at his watch. "I'm afraid I've got to get back to the city tonight, but I'll return in a few days. Perhaps I could persuade you to dine with me when I return."

He didn't wait for an answer but kissed my hand and slipped out the door. I didn't have a chance to decide if he was charming or overbearing before Pauline, the mayor's secretary, called my name, waving at me from the bar where she stood between Kyla and Jennifer.

She presented me with something green in a mason jar with a huge purple bow on top. "They're pickled peppers," she blurted out. "I make them myself. And before you ask, no, Peter Piper didn't pick them." She snorted at her own joke.

I managed a small chuckle for her benefit. "Thanks." I hated peppers, but maybe when they were pickled, the taste would be more tolerable.

"Oh, I love your peppers," Kyla said.

"Me, too," Jennifer said, her father no longer by her side.

I glanced around the room, but he must have left, not that I minded.

"Do you mind if I share them?" I asked Pauline.

"Of course not," she said, obviously proud of how popular her peppers were.

I opened the jar and reached in, pulling a pepper out and handing the rest to Kyla. She grabbed one and took a big bite, so I bravely nibbled at mine.

Blech. I swallowed the piece without chewing, chasing it with a swig of my drink. Tucking the pepper into the folds of a napkin, I watched Jennifer nibbling on one while Kyla gobbled up two more

Freddie glanced at her pager and sighed. "There's an emergency at the hospital. I'll be back as soon as I can."

I turned to Pauline. "I didn't know anyone still used pagers."

"The cell phone service is terrible along the water." She took one of her own peppers and bit into it, chewing happily. "Every month when the city council meets, the mayor tries to get approval to put in more cell towers, and every month, she gets voted down."

"Sounds like they don't like progress."

"It depends on what you consider progress. They'll bull-doze a historic building in a heartbeat if it suits their purpos-es." Pauline took another pepper, and I passed the jar on to the accountant and his friends.

THE NIGHT FLEW by as we ate, drank, and ate some more. After my third trip to the buffet, I headed back to my spot at the bar. Kyla passed me, rubbing her stomach.

"I'll be right back. At least I hope so." She gave me a weak smile. "I think I ate too many of those peppers. They're just so yummy."

I grimaced. "If you say so. Can I get you something? Some water maybe?"

"I'm sure I'll be fine." She formed the words carefully. "That second drink went right to my head. I think I'll get some fresh air."

"I'll come with you."

She waved me off. "No--go back to your party. I'll be fine."

As I approached the bar, Jennifer stood to give me her seat. She wobbled, holding onto the bar to steady herself.

"How much have you had to drink?" I asked.

"Just one. But it was pretty strong. I feel kinda woozy." She sat back down on the barstool and put her hands on her cheeks. "My face feels weird."

I knew she wasn't much of a drinker, and my lemon drop had been potent. Still, I didn't think she was *that* much of a lightweight. I turned to ask Pauline to keep an eye on Jennifer while I checked on Kyla, but Pauline's eyes drooped as if she had trouble staying awake.

"Are you okay?" I asked her.

"I think so," she said, before putting her hand over her mouth and running in the direction of the restroom.

I pulled out my cell phone to call Freddie, but the call wouldn't go through. Only a single, unsteady bar showed on the display.

Spotting Irma at the other end of the bar, I hurried over to her. "I need to use your phone."

Her brows knitted together with worry. "What's wrong?"

"I think some people have food poisoning."

"Impossible," she said. "I prepare my food—"

"Your phone," I repeated, louder this time, not wanting to waste time discussing Irma's food safety precautions.

"We need to call Freddie or the paramedics. Better yet, both."

Her eyes widened, no doubt hearing the panic in my voice. I followed her behind the bar to a tiny office.

Irma picked up the phone and gave me a puzzled look. "There's no dial tone."

"What do you mean?" I asked, grabbing the receiver from her and putting it up to my ear. The phone was out of order, and we had no way to get help for Kyla and the others. Food poisoning could be serious. Deadly serious.

IRMA GRABBED one of her bartenders as he walked in the back door ready to start his shift and sent him back out with urgent instructions to find a phone and call paramedics.

"Do you have internet access?" I asked Irma. "We could send Freddie a message."

"The phone and internet are on the same line. If the internet goes down, the phone does too, and vice versa. Do you really think it's food poisoning?"

"Yes, but I don't think your food made them sick. I had a big plateful of pretty much everything, and I'm fine."

"Then what?"

"Those darn peppers." I searched the room for anyone who seemed ill besides Kyla, Jennifer, and Pauline. Who else had eaten the peppers? I looked for the accountant and his friends, but they must have left early. Had they felt ill, too?

The front door swung open, and a tall, sturdy woman entered. I recognized the imposing figure of Mayor Wanda Gasden.

She haughtily surveyed the scene, appearing to search for someone in particular. Her eyes latched onto Pauline who'd found a seat near the back of the restaurant. The mayor headed toward her assistant who leaned back in her chair, her face pale.

"You're drunk," she accused Pauline.

"Hold on." I hurried over to Pauline to come to her defense. "She's not feeling well."

"You stay out of it," the mayor snapped at me before turning her attention back to Pauline. "I'm taking you home."

"You need to take her to the hospital," I said. "I think she has food poisoning."

"Food poisoning?" The mayor's voice rose so everyone could hear. "That's it. I'm shutting this place down for sure this time."

She grabbed Pauline, who chose just that moment to throw up on Mayor Gasden's expensive-looking pumps.

"Pauline!" the mayor cried out in a scolding tone. She grabbed a napkin from a nearby table and wiped off her shoes before dragging her assistant by one arm to the front door. As they exited, Freddie entered.

"What's going on?" Freddie asked when she saw the mayor and Pauline.

"I'm shutting this place down," the mayor yelled before kicking the front door open. She hauled Pauline outside and the door slammed behind her.

"I'm so glad you're back." I lowered my voice and told Freddie my theory. "I think Jennifer, Pauline, and Kyla may have contracted food poisoning from Pauline's pickled peppers."

Her eyes widened. "Botulism," she murmured, saying out loud what I'd already suspected. "Did you call an ambulance?"

Sirens faintly wailed, growing louder as the ambulance neared.

Relief washed over me. "Thank goodness. Everything's going to be okay."

Two paramedics entered, and Freddie took charge, directing them to attend to Jennifer while she checked on the other guests to see if there were other victims.

"Where's Kyla?" I asked Irma who'd slipped behind the bar to stay out of the way of the medical professionals.

She drew her brows together as her eyes scanned the room. "I haven't seen her for a while."

I hurried outside onto the dark patio but found it deserted. The steps leading to the parking lot were lit, so I headed in that direction, thinking maybe Kyla had gone home. I stopped and gasped. There at the bottom of the steps lay Kyla.

CHAPTER 5

I ran to Kyla's side and tried to rouse her, calling her name and shaking her shoulder. I touched her neck and felt a faint flutter of a pulse. No time to lose, I ran back inside to tell Freddie that Kyla needed her help.

Freddie barked an order to one of the paramedics, and they followed me to where Kyla lay unconscious. I stood nearby, watching nervously while they worked to revive her, finally putting her on a stretcher and taking her to the ambulance.

I called out after Freddie, "Will she be okay?" but she didn't answer.

When I returned to the party, the mood had turned somber, and most of the party guests had left. A few diners remained in their booths, not willing to let people being carted off on stretchers ruin their evening.

After Irma went from booth to booth explaining what had happened, she returned to her post behind the bar, absent-mindedly wiping glasses. She looked up as I approached. "I'm sorry about your party. I hope everyone is going to be okay."

I closed my eyes and said a silent prayer. "I'm going home to get my car and drive to the hospital." Adorable, sweet Jennifer. I didn't want to think of her lying in a hospital bed. She had to be okay.

"Call me with an update," Irma demanded, back to her usual bossy self. "Tonight. I won't sleep otherwise."

"Is your internet service back up?"

She glanced over her shoulder before leaning closer. "The connection had come loose," she said, her voice quiet. "Or someone unplugged it."

"But why would someone—" I paused. "Oh. Maybe someone didn't want us calling an ambulance." That would mean that someone wanted people to get sick or even die from Pauline's peppers. But how would they know that they were tainted? I looked around for the jar. "Where's the jar of peppers? Please tell me no one got rid of it."

Irma reached below the bar and retrieved the jar. Only one pepper remained along with a little juice. She found a paper bag and put the jar inside. "Are you going to have it tested?"

I nodded, but I felt sure I knew what Freddie would find.

I HURRIED ALONG SHORELINE ROAD, cursing my high heels, arriving home fifteen minutes later. As I unlocked my front door, my phone buzzed with a text from Jennifer. She'd been released from the hospital and her father had taken her home to spend the night at his house. She promised she'd be back the next day. I could only imagine how frantic with worry he must have been. I told her not to hurry back and suggested she take a few days to recuperate.

I draped the jacket she'd loaned me over the back of the sofa, so I didn't forget to return it. A cup of chamomile tea might calm my nerves and my mind, allowing me to think more clearly. I entered the kitchen and found Chef Emile leaning against the counter as if he'd been waiting up for me. As I filled up the electric kettle with filtered tap water, I told him about the food poisoning, thinking he might know something about botulism.

"Food safety is of paramount importance," he said. "There is no excuse for allowing food to become contaminated. One must wash one's hands regularly. All foods must be stored at the proper temperature and thrown out when it shows signs of deterioration, mold, or putrefaction."

"Ick." I wasn't in the mood for a lecture. "I know all about food safety and so does Irma. A jar of home-canned peppers was the culprit."

"Heaven save us from the home canner."

"Heaven help us from pickled peppers is more like it. I'm lucky I only took a bite."

Chef appeared to have lost interest in the conversation and gone back to his writing, so I brewed my cup of tea in silence. I couldn't stop thinking the tainted peppers hadn't been an accident, and I searched my mind for the reason I felt that way. The phone and internet going down at the Mermaid Cafe could have been an unfortunate coincidence, but I didn't think so.

The peppers had been given to me, but if anyone wanted to harm me, it would have been easy enough to find out that I hated peppers. If the poisoning had been done on purpose, I doubted I was the target.

"Do you like peppers?" I asked Chef. I didn't know how common they were in French cuisine.

His pen stopped and he turned toward me, no doubt sensing an opportunity to lecture me on a new subject. "Are you referring to *poivron rouge* or *piment rouge*?" When I responded with raised eyebrows, he translated. "*Poivron rouge* are what you Americans call red bell peppers, and *piment rouge* are épice … what is the word… Spicy. I understand they are quite popular in Mexican cooking."

"Chili peppers or cayenne? Or jalapeno?"

"The cayenne and the jalapeño are both varieties of chili pepper, and I use neither in my cooking. The flavors of French cuisine are subtle and refined, devoid of overpowering additives and seasonings."

"I see," I said. "Bland." I didn't find French cooking at all bland, but I hoped to get a rise out of him.

Just as I expected, he reacted visibly to my comment, his facial muscles tensing and his eyes narrowing. "Bland? You call the meticulous blending of the finest ingredients bland?"

I grinned in response, and he stormed off. When he did this, he appeared to walk through the walls, and I had no idea where he went. He claimed he never left the room, and I'd often wondered if the chef was destined to spend his afterlife in my kitchen.

I took my tea into the front room and plopped in front of the fireplace out of habit. Even without a fire burning, it was the coziest spot in the house. I sent Freddie a message asking about Kyla. Jennifer had recovered quickly, and I hoped Kyla would as well.

I sipped my tea and stared at the empty fireplace, lost in thought. A knock at the door brought me back to the present, and I waved Freddie in, too tired to get up.

"You should really keep the door locked," she scolded as she joined me on the sofa.

"What's the point? Anyone could break the glass and come right in. I've talked to Mark about putting in a security system, but there have been so many jobs to do getting the tearoom ready for opening, we haven't gotten around to it."

Freddie pulled out her phone and typed a message with

her thumbs. She stared at the screen until it buzzed, then put her phone away. "He'll be over tomorrow to take care of it."

"Okay, bossy," I teased, though I knew I'd feel safer once I had it installed. "I have something for you." I went into the kitchen, returning with the paper bag that held the pepper jar. "I figured you'd want to test this."

She took the bag and peered inside. "The symptoms all point to botulism, but I do want to confirm the source. You seem pretty sure it's from the peppers."

I sat back down on the sofa. "Look who got sick. Jennifer, Pauline, Kyla—they all ate the peppers. I didn't."

"The problem is botulism spores don't typically survive in pickled vegetables. The acidic pH kills them."

I tried to make sense of what she said. "I don't under-stand. I ate everything at the party except the peppers and I didn't get sick, while Kyla ate several pickles, and she seemed to be the sickest."

At the mention of Kyla, Freddie stared at her hands.

I waited for her to tell me what she had on her mind, though a part of me already knew. "Will Kyla be okay?"

She looked up at me, blinking back tears. She didn't have to say the words. I knew it.

Kyla was dead.

CHAPTER 6

*T*he morning brought clouds and drizzle, and I came downstairs to a chilly room. I'd been warned that June gloom would follow May gray and told not to expect regular sunshine until July. Using the gas log lighter Mark had installed, I started a fire and turned on a few lights.

I went into the kitchen to make a cup of instant coffee, missing my personal barista. I'd have to ask Jennifer to show me how to use the cappuccino machine. The enormous contraption worked surprisingly well despite its age, but the dials and knobs intimidated me.

I'd just filled the electric kettle when the doorbell rang, and I met Mark at the front door. "You didn't waste any time."

He stepped inside. "Doc wants to make sure you're safe. So do I."

His expression didn't indicate anything more than neighborly concern, so I did my best not to read more into his words.

"I'll be in the kitchen if you need me," I said, leaving him to his job. When I entered the kitchen, the back door opened, startling me. Jennifer appeared, wearing an oversized T-shirt and sweatpants, so unlike her usual style of dressing.

I grabbed her in a hug, then held her at arm's length. Dark circles under her eyes were the only evidence of her traumatic experience.

"I didn't expect you back so soon." I practically shoved her onto a stool. "Sit down. I'll make you breakfast."

She gave me a weak smile. "My dad made me breakfast. You should have seen him fussing over me."

I sat back down at the island across from her. "He must have been scared to death when he found out you were in the hospital with food poisoning."

She winced. "You don't know the half of it. My dad's been through a lot."

I knew the story. His mother had abandoned him, leaving him to be raised by an abusive father, Jennifer's grandfather. Then, when Jennifer was a teenager, she and her mother were in a car crash. Jennifer recovered after a long convalescence, but her mother didn't make it.

"I'm glad you're back, and not only because I hate instant coffee." I'd barely touched my cup and it had gone cold. When Jennifer made a move to stand up from her stool, I stopped her. "Don't you dare get up."

She waved a hand, dismissing my concern. "I'm fine." She stepped up to the cappuccino machine, flipping switches and filling the water tank. "They said I had a mild case, and I was lucky I hadn't eaten more of the peppers. Pauline went home last night, too." She hesitated, her mouth set tightly. "You heard about Kyla?"

I nodded, not trusting my voice.

"That could have been me, you know." She returned to the machine, preparing to pull two shots of espresso. "Thank goodness I only ate one of the peppers. That must have been what made us sick."

"But why did you recover so quickly while Kyla…" I couldn't finish the sentence. "And Pauline ate at least two, but you say she's fine now. I know Kyla ate three or four, but I just don't understand why she became so much sicker than anyone else."

Jennifer shrugged as the steamer hissed. She expertly layered the foamy milk on top of the espresso, and handed me my drink, returning to her seat at the island. "Things like that affect people differently, I guess. Like how I can drink coffee all day long and still get to sleep, and you can't have even one cup after lunch, or you'll be up all night."

The heart she'd formed in the foam made me smile. "That's because you're young. I used to be able to do a lot of things when I was your age."

"Maybe that's why I bounced back so quickly from this."

My gut told me there was more to it. Everyone knew Kyla had been digging up secrets for her novel, and some people might not want their dirty laundry to be exposed. With Kyla dead, would the manuscript ever see the light of day?

Jennifer must have noticed my preoccupation. "What's bothering you?"

"You mean besides Kyla?" I didn't want to share my suspicions with her yet. "I've got a lot on my mind. On top of everything, I've still got a grand opening fundraiser to plan. And don't even think about working today," I said, before she had a chance to object. "I expect you to curl up with a good book and relax."

"I guess I'll go upstairs," she said glumly as if she'd been sent to her room without supper.

"Oh, I almost forgot." I retrieved the jacket she'd loaned me. "Thanks again for making me look so good yesterday and loaning me this." I handed her the jacket.

Jennifer took it, headed for the stairs, but stopped.

"There's something in the pocket." She pulled out the birthday card Kyla had given me.

"Thanks, I'd forgotten about that. It's from Kyla, and I haven't even read it yet." I sighed and opened the envelope. The card had a teacup on the front and the spa gift card she'd told me about inside. I read her note. "To a good friend. Love, Kyla." I blinked, trying to keep from crying. I barely had a chance to get to know her, and now I never would.

Jennifer pulled out something else and handed it to me. "Did someone give you a flash drive?"

I stared at the device. "No."

"Well, it's not mine, so it must be yours." She took her cup and climbed the stairs to her room, probably planning to read *Pride and Prejudice* for the umpteenth time.

I put the flash drive in my pocket. I'd figure out who it belonged to later. I had work to do.

A FEW HOURS LATER, Jennifer came downstairs, claiming boredom. She kept me company while I baked vanilla cream fruit tarts. I planned to offer them along with afternoon tea.

Jennifer looked up from her cup of tea. "April?"

I gave her my best motherly glare. "For the last time, no, you can't help."

"Your phone is buzzing."

"Oh." I picked up my phone, but the call had already gone to voicemail. I listened to the message. The new acting police chief, Deputy Alex Molina, wanted me to come to the station and answer some questions. I pulled off my apron and let Jennifer know where I was going.

"Do you think it's about Kyla's death and the peppers?" she asked.

"Must be." Not bothering to explain what Freddie had

told me about pickled vegetables not being a natural source of the toxin, I found my purse and keys and warned her not to do any work while I was gone.

The police station took up several rooms adjacent to our city hall. I hadn't met Deputy Molina and had hoped we wouldn't have a reason to meet at all. My experience with the former police chief had been less than positive.

Once inside, I headed for Pauline's desk. She worked for the mayor, but our town being so small, she also assisted the police chief. I wanted to find out if she had any information about Kyla's death. When she saw me coming, she jumped up from her chair and ran over to me, grabbing me in a hug.

When she released me, she began apologizing. "I'm so sorry. I don't know what happened with the peppers. I always follow safe food handling procedures, and I've never had a single problem before. I'm devastated. Did you hear about Kyla?"

I nodded, but before I could say anything, she went on.

"I'm heartbroken. Just heartbroken." She returned to her desk and fell into her chair as if she had no more strength to stay upright.

"Where did you keep the peppers before you brought them to my party?" I asked.

She tilted her head, as if confused. "They were here. I worked that day, but the mayor let me take off early for your party."

"When you say here, do you mean at your desk?"

She blinked nervously and nodded. "They don't require refrigeration." Her voice sounded defensive.

A male voice behind me interrupted my questioning. "April May?"

I turned to see a medium height, broad-shouldered man in a grey suit scowling in my direction. He narrowed his dark eyes. I'm sure he meant to intimidate me with his glare, but he didn't look more than thirty years old, and I had a sudden urge to pinch his chubby cheeks.

"I'm the acting police chief, Deputy Alex Molina." He pushed a lock of jet-black hair from his forehead and motioned for me to follow him.

His austere office held a metal desk, a filing cabinet, and no signs of personality. He motioned for me to take a seat in a folding chair before settling in behind his desk. A single picture showed a lovely woman with long, dark hair holding an infant. I recognized the deputy's chubby cheeks on the child.

"Is that your wife and baby?" I asked.

A hint of a smile crossed his face as he nodded, then he was back to being all business. "I brought you here to ask some questions about your party last night. There's some uncertainty surrounding the events, so the coroner has deemed Kyla Bradley's death suspicious until all the evidence is gathered."

He didn't sound particularly motivated to investigate her death, and I wondered why not. Picking up a pen, he made some marks on the pad of paper on his desk. I wondered if they were doodles.

"I understand you were gifted a jar of peppers."

"Yes, Pauline gave them to me, but I don't really like peppers, so—"

"If you would please just answer the questions, this will go much faster."

I nodded and waited to see what else he wanted to know. I had hoped that Deputy Molina would be an improvement over our previous police chief, Sergeant Rawley, but I began to lose hope in his abilities. I didn't care for his attitude either.

"As well as you can remember, who ate the peppers?"

I listed Jennifer, Pauline, and Kyla. "Kyla ate the most, I

believe. And there were three men, Irma's accountant and his two friends who might have had some, but they left before the others began to feel ill."

"But the peppers were given to you. Why didn't you eat any?"

"I hate peppers. I ate a tiny bite just to be polite." He'd said to only answer the questions, so I didn't elaborate.

He stared at the paper as if unsure what to ask next.

"Was it botulism?" I asked.

He looked up and raised his eyebrows, but didn't answer my question.

I had another one. "Do you think the poisoning was intentional?"

His eyes widened with apparent surprise. "Is there something you know?"

"No," I quickly replied. "I just thought since you were investigating…" Kyla had told me someone didn't want the book published, and now she was dead. I didn't have anything concrete to tell the deputy, and I didn't think he'd take me seriously anyway.

"You need to trust me," Molina said, looking me straight in the eye. "Do you understand?"

I didn't understand. I didn't even know him, so why would I trust him?

He tapped his pen on the notepad. "Do you think someone might have wanted to harm Kyla?"

I paused a moment too long. "If so, it's because of the novel she was writing."

He scoffed. "Who would kill someone over a book? It's fiction, right? And no one seems to know if she ever finished it." He raised an eyebrow. "Any other theories?"

"If I had any real knowledge, I'd tell you." I hesitated. "You want me to trust you, but I don't think you trust me."

"I'd have no trouble trusting people if they would only tell me the truth."

I left him sitting at his desk, no doubt working on his doodles. The acting police chief didn't have much to keep him busy, since not much happened in this town. Well, other than an occasional murder.

CHAPTER 7

*B*efore leaving the police station, I gave Freddie a call. She was home and invited me to stop by. The sun hung low over the ocean as I turned down her street and pulled up in front of her storybook cottage.

Freddie opened the front door wearing an oversized cream-colored sweater and leggings, her hair in a topknot. She invited me into her comfy living room. "Have you eaten?"

"I can wait until I get home." It wasn't like me to forget to eat, but since learning of Kyla's death I didn't have much of an appetite. "I wouldn't mind a glass of wine if you have one."

Freddie disappeared into the kitchen and returned with a plate of crackers and cheese and two glasses of wine. "No wine unless you eat something," she said in a mock-scolding voice.

I took the offered snack gratefully. "I just came from an interview with Deputy Molina. He said you think Kyla's death was suspicious."

Freddie sat on an overstuffed chair across from me. "It's a preliminary determination. Until the post-mortem, we don't have enough information to make a conclusion about Kyla's death."

"But the tests showed botulism, right? The symptoms seemed consistent." I'd looked up the effects of botulism—shortness of breath, difficulty swallowing or speaking, abdominal distress for starters. "If it wasn't the peppers that poisoned everyone, then what? I'm pretty sure I tried everything on the buffet." I racked my brain, trying to remember if I'd skipped any dishes. "I didn't eat much of the coleslaw, but that would be acidic, too, wouldn't it?"

She took a sip of wine. "I don't think anyone got sick from Irma's food. I found toxin in the pickle jar."

Now I felt lost. "But I thought you said that pickled vegetables didn't normally harbor botulism. The acidic pH killed it, or something like that."

"That's right." Hiding her emotions behind her firm, steady voice, she explained. "The tests on the pickle jar showed a purified form of botulism—botulinum toxin, the sort that dermatologists and cosmetic surgeons inject under the skin to relax muscles and get rid of crow's feet and frown lines."

I blinked, trying to process her meaning. "Someone injected the pickles with it?"

"Either that or they put the toxin in the jar with the pepper juice. The thing is, Kyla's blood levels were ten times what we found in Jennifer. I haven't gotten the results back from Pauline's blood test yet, but considering her relatively mild symptoms, I'm guessing her levels will be similar to Jennifer's."

"So how did Kyla get such a large dose?" What if someone put toxin in the jar of peppers to make her death appear accidental? "Do you think Kyla got an extra dose somehow?"

Freddie nodded. "Yes."

That could only mean one thing. "You think Kyla was murdered."

She lowered her head. "I do."

"How could it have happened?" I wondered out loud. "Did someone inject Kyla with the toxin? You would have seen a mark. Was there a mark?"

She shook her head. "No needle marks."

I picked up my wineglass, pausing before I took a sip. "In her drink? No, she would have tasted it. Or would she? Does botulinum toxin have a taste?"

"No, it doesn't," she said. "Did you see who had access to her drink?"

I closed my eyes, picturing the scene in my mind. Her drink had been on the bar, and I'd sat with my back to it. We'd all stood or sat with our backs to the bar. "Our drinks were on the bar, and there were plenty of people around. Any of them could have slipped something in her drink, I suppose."

"Or the poisoning could have happened earlier in the day. Botulism would take hours before having any effect, although being a purified version of the poison, it might have acted more quickly. There aren't a lot of cases to reference." She leaned back in her chair, scowling in frustration. "I don't know how we're going to track down who poisoned Kyla. Although I think we both have an idea of why."

I nodded. "The tell-all book she was writing."

"I suggested to Deputy Molina that he might want to search her home to look for it on her computer, but he seems reluctant to treat Kyla's death as anything but an unfortunate accident."

"I got that feeling when he questioned me," I said. "Has anyone seen a copy of the book? Maybe she sent it to a publisher or agent."

"I don't know anyone who's seen even a paragraph, but everyone seems to think they know what's in it."

"And what do they say?" I asked.

"No one's given me any specific details, but there are plenty of rumors. It seems as though everyone in this town has secrets."

If everyone had secrets, that meant everyone had a motive to kill Kyla.

CHAPTER 8

I woke Wednesday morning in a panic. Only ten days until the grand opening reception, which didn't feel like enough time. The tense feeling in my stomach convinced me I must have forgotten an important task.

On top of everything, I felt I owed it to Kyla to find out who had poisoned her. Deputy Molina didn't seem to be in a big hurry to solve the case. Thank goodness we had Freddie as our coroner, or someone might have gotten away with murder.

As I slipped into the pants I'd worn the day before, I felt the flash drive in the pocket. I placed it on my dresser and made my way downstairs, stepping quietly so I didn't wake Jennifer. With my mind in a jumble, some fresh air might help clear my head. I grabbed my notebook with the to-do list and stepped onto the front porch, only to be greeted by a blast of cold air. Across the street, the waves crashed wildly, throwing spray into the air.

Despite the gloomy weather we'd had since I moved to town, I loved living across the street from the beach. I doubted I would ever get tired of listening to the crashing waves and inhaling the salty air. After ducking back inside for a jacket, I settled on the porch swing. As I swayed back and forth, I checked off the completed tasks. I'd hired a caterer who would bring additional servers to assist Jennifer and me, rented mannequins to display Irma's dresses and the jewelry, placed an ad in the local paper promoting the event, and sent out a slew of press releases.

I hadn't yet found anyone to host the evening's festivities in Kyla's place. Irma might agree to do it, but one never knew quite what to expect from her. The task would likely fall to me if I couldn't find someone soon, but I'd be busy with everything else and would rather not have to be the emcee for the night too.

A burgundy Aston Martin convertible stopped in front of my house, and a tall man in jeans and a pullover sweater stepped out. The day was taking a turn for the better.

He smiled and waved as if he knew me, then strolled my way. It was Sebastian, the man I'd met at my party. I returned his smile and said hello.

"May I?" He gestured to the seat next to me.

I stood. "Why don't you come inside where it's warm, and I'll make a pot of coffee."

He followed me inside, stopping just inside the door. "Oh my. You've done a marvelous job transforming this place. It reminds me of the tearoom at the Biltmore. Have you been?"

I grinned. "That was part of my inspiration." Taking off my jacket, I shivered in the cold room. "Let me start the fire, then I'll put the coffee on. How do you take it?"

"Black for me. And I can take care of the fire if you like," he said.

"That would be lovely." I enjoyed having a man around, even occasionally, but what was he doing here? I attempted to ignore the butterflies in my stomach, remembering how pompous he seemed when we'd met.

Jennifer surprised me in the kitchen, since I hadn't realized she'd come downstairs.

"I'll make your friend an Americano," she said, obviously having overheard Sebastian's request. "What about you? Mocha?"

"I'm saving those for special occasions, like Mondays," I said with a chuckle. "Too many calories."

When I returned with our coffee mugs, I took a seat on the sofa in front of a roaring fire.

"I hope you don't mind me stopping by." He took a seat in the chair next to me. "I forgot to ask for your number, and I couldn't find your information online. I'm surprised you don't have a website."

I jumped up. "The website! I knew there was something I was forgetting." I grabbed my notebook and flipped to my to-do list, adding "finish website," in large letters. I sat down again, giving him an embarrassed smile. "I feel better now that you've reminded me."

"I heard through the grapevine you're planning a fundraiser to reopen the library. I'd love to help in any way I can. I spent a lot of time there when I was growing up."

"That's right, you said you were renovating your family home. I should have known you'd grown up here."

"My father passed away when I was ten years old. I loved my mother, and I believe she loved me, but she had social duties—charities to run and foundations, things like that. I don't think she knew what to do with a young boy."

"I'm sorry," I said.

He shook his head. "That's very kind, but I had a privileged upbringing. No child has everything they need, wouldn't you agree?"

Thinking about my own childhood, I agreed. "That's so true."

"Every day after school, I'd stop by the library and spend the afternoon reading. I found family and friends in books. They were so much more interesting than the people I knew in real life. The librarians talked to me about books, telling me about ones they enjoyed and setting aside favorites for me to read. They were like family to me. So, you see, I wasn't deprived."

I couldn't help but think that literary characters and librarians were no substitute for the attention of your own mother, but I kept that opinion to myself.

He leaned back in his chair and took a drink of his coffee. "You can probably understand why I have a special feeling for the library. I'd love to help with the fundraiser any way I can."

"Thanks for the offer." There was something he could do. "Would you consider being the emcee for the event?" Before he could answer, I added, "I know it's a lot to ask, it's just that Kyla had agreed to do it…"

"I'd be happy to." He gave me a genuine smile, convincing me he meant it. "I didn't know Kyla personally, but she seemed like a lovely lady. It's so sad for her to have died from something preventable like food poisoning."

I stared at my coffee cup. He didn't need to know that Kyla had likely been murdered. The whole town would find out soon enough.

"I'm sorry," he said. "Did you know her well?"

"I thought I had all the time in the world to know her better." Tears unexpectedly welled, and I did my best to blink them back. "I just moved to town, but she made me feel welcome, and I'll always be grateful for that."

We sat in silence for a few moments before Sebastian spoke again. "Why don't I take you to dinner tomorrow evening, and we can talk about the fundraiser? I'd rather not go to the Mermaid Cafe, if you don't mind. After being away for so long, I'm afraid we'd get interrupted and have no time to ourselves."

The only other restaurants were a pizza place, a taco stand, and the unexceptional hotel dining room. "Why don't we have dinner here?" I suggested. "Then we won't have any interruptions."

"That would be delightful," he said. "But only on one condition—I do the cooking."

It had been a long time since a man cooked for me, and I quickly agreed.

"And the shopping," he added.

"What do I need to do?"

"I believe you have a website to complete," he said with a grin. "I'll see you at six tomorrow evening, if that works for you."

That worked for me perfectly.

WHILE JENNIFER SPENT the day polishing woodwork and dusting, I spent the day in front of the computer, taking breaks only for lunch and dinner, and I finally published the website just before bedtime. As I changed into pajamas, the flash drive I'd left on top of the dresser caught my eye. I picked it up and headed to my parlor, where my laptop sat on a table with a view of the ocean.

While waiting for the computer to boot up, I turned the flash drive over in my hand. Nothing indicated what files, if any, might be stored on it. I plugged it into the USB port and pulled up the list of files on my screen.

The file names showed little rhyme or reason. One appeared to be recipes and another research. I clicked on the file titled Balmy Bay.

Secrets of Balmy Bay it said at the top of the page, with

Kyla Bradley listed as the author. This was Kyla's novel, the one that might have gotten her killed, and now I had a copy —possibly the only copy. She must have slipped it in my pocket at the party, but why?

"In the idyllic burgh of Balmy Bay, secrets abound," I read. "The community appears wholesome and friendly, but underneath the tranquil surface, wickedness and depravity lurk."

I blinked, taken aback by Kyla's flair for the dramatic. Wickedness and depravity? I read on, skimming several paragraphs describing Balmy Bay in elaborate detail and leaving no doubt it was a thinly veiled version of Serenity Cove.

The next chapter caught my interest. She wrote about two sisters whose father had built a home for them to share —each floor a complete residence including parlor, bedrooms, and kitchen. She'd changed the sisters' names, but she obviously referred to my house and the Thornly Sisters, the first residents of my home.

The Thatcher sisters fought from the time they could form words. Perhaps their father hoped that providing them with a domicile to share would heal their fractured relationship, but it was not to be. Bessie, considered to be a handsome woman, couldn't compete with the ravishing and cunning Natalie.

Their father departed this realm just at the time the two girls reached womanhood. Bessie married at the age of nineteen, undoubtedly pleased to be away from the machinations of her sister. Natalie, meanwhile, freed from the strict oversight of her older sister, became as wild as an untamed mustang. She flaunted her shapely figure and used her father's money to adorn herself in silk and jewels.

I yawned, finding Kyla's prose overwrought and difficult to read, especially at this late hour. I skimmed ahead past the history of the sisters until I came to a part about a handsome chef who Natalie lured to her new restaurant. According to the story, they were lovers.

Chef Emile Toussaint had admitted to me he'd once been in love with Norma, but claimed his feelings weren't reciprocated, and I had no reason to doubt him. Despite that error in her story, I marveled at how many other details Kyla had gotten right, although most of the people involved were long dead. I skipped ahead several pages, looking for a more recent story involving one of the living residents. The people in town weren't likely to be worried about Kyla publishing historical fiction based on long dead townspeople.

I nearly missed a mention of Ida, a teenaged girl originally from Puerto Rico loosely based on Irma. I read with interest, wondering how Kyla had learned so much about my irascible new friend. She even included the detail that Norma gave Irma the previous year's designer dresses so she would be presentable as the restaurant's hostess. That didn't seem like the sort of information anyone would want to keep secret.

And then it got interesting.

Young Ida met a handsome carpenter and fell in love. Engaged to be married, she believed her future happiness was assured until the duplicitous Natalie stole her fiancé. Parading a diamond ring around town, Natalie took every opportunity to humiliate her rival.

When Ida found herself with child by her erstwhile sweetheart, Norma suggested she leave and have her baby elsewhere, asserting that the baby's father-to-be agreed. The suggestion was amplified by a large payoff.

Was this true? Irma had said she'd left town to have her baby. It broke my heart to think she'd been betrayed in such a cruel way.

Barely able to keep my eyes open, I turned off the computer. I hadn't found any clues hinting at who had murdered Kyla, but I thought it prudent to hide the flash drive with her manuscript. If she'd been concerned enough to slip it to me, I might as well make sure nothing happened to it until I had a chance to read more.

Somewhere in Kyla's novel might be a motive for murder.

CHAPTER 9

The next morning when I woke, the laptop beckoned to me. Sebastian would be coming over to cook me dinner that night, and I wanted to re-organize my chaotic kitchen before he arrived. But first, I read one more of Kyla's stories.

In the mid-eighties, Balmy Bay experienced a superfluity of offspring born to local residents. Even the Robinsons, who had abandoned their quest for parenthood, found themselves blessed with offspring—two healthy baby girls. The Robinson sisters' childhood was uneventful, though hints of trouble began to surface when the girls reached their teens. While Roberta comported herself in an acceptable manner and followed the dictums of common decency, her sister Cheryl exasperated her parents with her reckless and rebellious ways.

When the girls obtained maturity, the Robinsons relinquished their Balmy Bay bungalow to their daughters while they relocated to a locale far away, washing their hands of the situation.

I skimmed ahead to see if it got more interesting.

Cheryl became heavy with child, though the identity of the father was not disclosed. Sadly, motherhood did not tame the wild sister. She attempted to sell her baby, undoubtedly seeking money to purchase drugs.

Sentenced to a psychiatric hospital where she spent the next ten years, Cheryl later returned to Balmy Bay. On her reappearance, she appeared to be a new person, both physically and mentally.

I skipped to the end of the sisters' story and read the sad conclusion.

One dark, moonless night, Cheryl leapt off the Balmy Bay lighthouse. Her broken body was found the next morning.

I closed the file and shut off my laptop, disturbed by the unsatisfying ending. That was the problem with real life—it didn't always come with a happy ending.

JENNIFER WAITED for me at the kitchen island with a perky smile meant to convince me that she'd fully recovered from her poisoning. I had to admit she appeared in perfect health.

She hopped off her stool and practically skipped over to the cappuccino machine. "What do we have planned for the day?"

"Sebastian Bernini has agreed to host the fundraiser at our grand opening. He's going to make dinner tonight, and I thought I'd straighten out the cupboards if you want to help."

"He's making you dinner?" she said with a teasing note. "He's very handsome."

I appreciated that she didn't add "for an old guy." He must have seemed ancient to her, but she was right about him being handsome. "Do you know him?"

"Not really," she said. "I was really little when he lived here. After his mom died, he left town. I think his dad died a long time ago, so his mom was all he had. He didn't visit much after that."

"That's sad." I knew how he felt, since I'd lost my mother a few months earlier. I'd never known my dad. "How about pancakes?"

Jennifer grinned. "I never say no to pancakes."

After breakfast, we pulled everything out of the kitchen cabinets and set the pots and pans, utensils, and all the other cooking equipment on the counters and island. We scrubbed the shelves and put down new shelf paper before putting everything back in what I hoped would be a more intuitive arrangement.

We did the same with the storage room that held the pantry, more cooking equipment, and the walk-in freezer. Not only did it feel good to clean and organize everything for the first time since I'd moved in, but now I knew where to find everything.

I'd grown up in a home where a single paring knife served about twenty different functions, and if you didn't have a tool or utensil, you improvised.

"I've worked up an appetite," I said, as we put the finishing touches on the storage area. "Chef has a recipe for French onion soup I've been wanting to try. How does that sound?"

"You make it," Jennifer grinned, "and I'll eat it. Do you want me to help?"

"We just got another shipment of supplies. Napkins and flatware, I think. I can't keep track of it all anymore."

Jennifer grabbed a clipboard from a hook on the wall. "That's why we have our order list. You're more organized than you think. I'll go see what's arrived and unpack it. Call me when lunch is ready, please."

HAVING a French chef living in my house, even if he was a ghost, meant that I had a freezer full of broth ready to whip up a quick bowl of soup. He'd taught me that having home-made broth on hand gave me a head start for many dishes. Add to that the ability to whip up basic French sauces, and I could prepare a gourmet meal in no time.

I had frozen the broth in silicon containers that were like trays for oversized ice cubes. Each one held a cup, just right for a bowl of soup or two. Stock also added flavor to polenta or grains when used instead of water, as the chef had taught me.

While Emile watched, I flipped through one of the cookbooks he had written and stopped when I found the right page. "I've decided to try your recipe for French onion soup. What do you think?"

"As you wish." His bored tone made me wonder what else he had to do while spending eternity in my kitchen.

"I can do it on my own if you're too busy."

"Forgive me," he said, not trying to hide his sarcasm. "Did I not display the proper amount of enthusiasm? Do you have any idea how many times I've made onion soup? Just throw some onions in the pan and let's get it over with."

What had gotten into him? Normally, he hovered over every dish, fussed over every step, every detail, expecting me to do the same.

"Are you okay?" I asked.

"What are you waiting for?" he asked, ignoring my question. "Start slicing."

I sliced the onions and added them to melted butter in my pan. I checked the recipe, which said to caramelize the onions over medium. "How long do they take to caramelize?"

"Thirty minutes or so."

"Thirty minutes? I have to stand here and stir for that long?"

He sighed. "No, you don't have to. You may throw the raw

onions in some broth if you like and see how they taste. It is all the same to me."

I stirred the onions silently while the chef sulked in the corner. The aroma of onions began to fill the kitchen, making my mouth water. I breathed in the scent and sighed. "That smells so good."

Chef looked up with an expression filled with such sadness it broke my heart. Did his sullen mood have to do with not being able to smell or taste the food he showed me how to cook? I should be grateful for my five senses and all the wonderful ingredients available not to mention a huge kitchen to work in.

I glanced at the clock, but I'd only been stirring for three minutes. The time would go faster if I could get the chef to tell me some of his stories.

"I'd love to hear more about Norma," I prompted. "She sounds like quite a remarkable woman."

He stared out the kitchen window and didn't answer right away. "Norma was a beautiful woman, but only on the outside. It took many years for me to see how she manipulated men, including me. Especially me."

"I'm sorry. Sometimes it's hard when you learn the truth about someone."

"I fear I was too easily swayed by charm and a pretty face." He turned back to me. "Now I realize there are more important qualities to be found in a woman such as kindness and loyalty."

"And a great sense of humor," I said, giving him a wink. "Don't forget that. It helps keep things interesting."

"Ah yes," he said with a little smile. "You do love your little jokes."

"Did you know Norma's sister Barbara too? Did they get along?"

"Now you make another joke," he scoffed. "They were like

oil and vinegar, except that if you shook them up, they were more likely to explode rather than make a vinaigrette for the salad course."

I asked him more questions about Norma until he motioned to let me know the onions were caramelized. The rest of the process went quickly. I added garlic, white wine, and beef stock, along with some herbs, and let it reduce for another fifteen minutes. All that was left to do was pour the soup into bowls, top them with a slice of toasted baguette and cheese, and put them under the broiler.

"Voila!" I said proudly. "Lunch is served."

Emile appeared uninterested. Considering he couldn't consume the meal, I didn't blame him. Hopefully, Jennifer would appreciate my efforts.

AFTER LUNCH, Jennifer finished unpacking supplies and set up a staging area just outside the kitchen for table settings. She had another bowl of French onion soup for dinner, turning down my invitation to join Sebastian and me.

When the doorbell rang, Jennifer said, "Have fun," and disappeared up the stairs.

Sebastian entered, carrying several grocery bags, and followed me to the kitchen. He placed them on the counter and began removing items—a bottle of wine, a tin of cannellini beans, fresh basil, and something wrapped in white paper.

Chef Emile leaned against the far counter, not looking our way. He didn't fool me—he paid attention to everything. I only hoped he'd stay quiet and not distract me.

"Sablefish," Sebastian said, holding up the package. "Also known as butterfish or black cod. The recipe calls for Chilean sea bass, but not only is it endangered from overfishing, it also tends to have high mercury levels. I've tried alternatives, and sablefish is my favorite."

"I'm looking forward to trying it." My mouth watered at the thought.

"I thought you might enjoy an authentic Italian meal."

"Ha!" Chef said, startling me. "The only thing authentic about this man is his hair, and I'm not even sure about that."

At this, Emile stepped up behind Sebastian. As I watched, horrified, he reached up, and tugged a lock of his hair.

Sebastian's eyes widened, and he touched the top of his head. It was all I could do not to squeal.

"What was that?" he asked.

"Must have been a draft." It was the best I could come up with at a moment's notice. "These old houses are so poorly insulated, that you can practically feel the wind sweeping through the rooms." What was I supposed to tell him? I could hardly say it was my not-so-friendly kitchen ghost.

As soon as I could, I gave Emile a stern look. I was not about to let him ruin my evening. "Italy and France aren't that far from each other. Is their cuisine that different?"

"Sacre bleu!" Chef exclaimed.

Sebastian smiled indulgently. "French food is all about the preparation, the work that goes into creating a dish. Italians believe that the food is delicious because of nature. An Italian chef will bring out the flavor in a way that highlights the taste rather than obscuring it."

"I see." It made a lot of sense to me.

"The freshest, highest quality ingredients make the best dishes. The French chef believes the food is delicious because of him."

"Bof!" Chef straightened up, his eyes darting from Sebastian back to me. "Does the fish leap from the ocean onto the pan and cook itself?"

I gave Chef a quick glare, then turned back to my real,

live guest. "Let me know what you need. I've got pretty much every type of pot, pan, and cooking utensil known to man. When I bought this house, the kitchen came fully stocked. I'm still learning what some of the contraptions do."

He looked around the sizable room, his eyes resting on the chopping board I'd laid out with a selection of knives nearby. "How about a can opener and a medium saucepan?"

"Easy-peasy." I retrieved the items he'd asked for and placed them on the counter. "What can I do to help?"

He handed me a container with chopped tomatoes and other ingredients. "If you'd like to plate the salad, I'll start the cannellini beans."

As olive oil heated in the saucepan, Sebastian chopped ingredients while I pulled salad plates from the cabinets. Fresh ingredients were not only tasty but also a feast for the eyes. The bright red tomatoes contrasted with white slices of onion and green herbs.

Chef stood next to me. "The freshest ingredients? Bah!"

I gestured to the salad and whispered, "What are you talking about?"

"What's that?" Sebastian asked.

I gave him a smile. "The salad looks beautiful."

Chef scowled. "The beans are canned."

I gave him a gesture to leave me alone, not wanting Sebastian to think I talked to myself. I supposed most people did, but not when they were with other people.

Sebastian added the garlic to the pan then the drained beans.

"Would you stir the beans while I make the sauce?" he asked, handing me the wooden spoon.

"Of course. I'm enjoying having company in the kitchen." I stuck my tongue out at Chef Emile, who narrowed his eyes at me.

"I'm guessing the house didn't come with a food processor." Sebastian knit his brows. "I should have thought of that."

I opened a cabinet door and gestured inside. "I wasn't going to run a tearoom without one. It's such a time saver." I took it out and placed it on the counter, plugging it in. "This and the microwave were the only appliances I had to buy."

Sebastian added basil, olive oil, garlic and a few other ingredients to the food processor, and pulsed it until he'd created a smooth basil sauce. Next, he seasoned the beans with salt and pepper, then used a potato masher to crush them gently.

Chef continued to watch us, despite the warning looks I shot him with each comment. "Peasant food," he smirked. "How lovely."

Sebastian put the lid on the saucepan. "Those should stay warm until we're ready for them." After seasoning and lightly flouring the fish fillets, he sauteed them in olive oil.

I handed him two dinner plates, and he placed a scoop of cannellini mash on them, topping it with the fish. Lastly, he drizzled on the sauce and scattered a few basil leaves on top.

My stomach growled at the sight, and I hoped he hadn't heard it. "That looks good enough to eat!"

Sebastian picked up the wine bottle and his plate. "Lead the way."

With one last glance at Chef Emile, I picked up my plate and led Sebastian to the table I'd set by the bay window.

"*Buon appetito.*" Sebastian reached out his glass to touch mine.

I broke off a large, delicate flake of the sablefish and took the first bite. The smooth, velvety texture nearly melted in my mouth. The subtle seasonings highlighted the taste of the fish. "This is wonderful."

While we ate, Sebastian told me more about what

Serenity Cove had been like when he was young. He seemed to have mixed feelings about growing up in a small town.

"It sounds like Serenity Cove hasn't changed much over the decades," I said, taking another sip of my wine.

"I guess it hasn't," he agreed. "Not in any of the important ways. But I'm glad for one change."

"What's that?" I asked.

"I'm glad that Serenity Cove now includes you."

CHAPTER 10

*A*fter Sebastian and I said goodnight, I climbed the steps to the upstairs parlor which I'd turned into my office. Situated in the front of the house, it had a huge window overlooking the road below and the ocean beyond. It made a perfect spot for running my business, at least the paperwork and numbers part of it.

While spending time with Sebastian, Kyla's murder had gone to the back of my mind. Now alone, I felt a strong urge to know who had a secret so volatile that they would kill to protect it.

Once I'd turned on the computer, I opened Kyla's file again with her manuscript and paged to the location I'd stopped reading the night before.

A year almost to the day, Ida returned. Accepting the money meant leaving and giving up her baby, but she had never agreed to stay away forever. The bribe allowed Ida to open her own restaurant, assuring her independence.

Natalie, furious at Ida's return, vowed to make life difficult for her, but nothing she did seemed to affect Ida. The feud went on for many years, and the passage of time didn't diminish their animosity, even when Natalie's husband, Ida's former love, passed away.

One day, Ida, now in her forties, visited Natalie, ostensibly to discuss a truce between them. The next visitor found Natalie at the bottom of the stairs, dead.

When the police couldn't prove she'd murdered Natalie, Ida went on with her life as if nothing had happened. Not surprisingly, she was not invited to Natalie's funeral.

THE NEXT MORNING, I sat at the island staring at my coffee cup.

"Late night with Sebastian?" Jennifer asked, a twinkle in her eye.

"Huh?" I blinked a few times. "Not really. I stayed up reading and lost track of the time."

"That happens to me all the time," Jennifer said. "What are you reading?"

I didn't want to lie, but I didn't want anyone to know I had Kyla's manuscript until I knew what incriminating information she'd uncovered. I said the first thing that came to mind. "Pride and Prejudice."

Jennifer's eyes lit up. "Isn't it wonderful? How far did you get?"

Luckily, I'd seen the movie so I could fake it. "I'm just where they meet Mr. Bingley." I didn't have to worry, because Jane Austin was one of Jennifer's favorite subjects, and she spent the next half hour giving me a synopsis of each of Austin's books including rating them. Pride and Prejudice was number one, of course.

When Jennifer went out to run errands, I gave Deputy Molina a call. The call went to voicemail, so I called Pauline.

"He's here, but he's on the phone," she informed me. "Is there a message?"

"Tell him I'm on my way to see him," I said. "I just need a few minutes of his time."

On the drive to the police station, I rehearsed what to tell Molina. I wanted him to know that Kyla may have been killed over her manuscript, but I didn't want him to know I had a copy. Not yet. For all I knew it was the only copy.

One of the secrets in Kyla's book might have gotten her killed, but that didn't mean all the secrets she wrote about needed to become common knowledge. I wanted to protect my friends. Some secrets could ruin someone's career or even their life if they became common knowledge.

After a short drive, I pulled into the parking lot next to City Hall. A minute later, I entered Deputy Molina's spartan office.

"Hello, Ms. May," he said in greeting. "What did you want to speak to me about?"

As soon as I took a seat across the desk from him, I didn't know what to say. I took a deep breath and tried to gather my thoughts. "I think Kyla was killed because of the book she was writing."

He nodded, and I wondered if he had come to the same conclusion. "Go on."

"Before she died, Kyla told me about a murder that happened in Serenity Cove a while ago. I think she wrote about it. I could tell she was afraid what someone might be willing to do to keep the book from being published."

"Afraid for her life?" he asked.

"I think so."

"That might explain why we weren't able to find the manuscript on her computer or in her home. Someone else might have been looking for it as well, since it appears her home had been searched before we arrived." He gave me a long look. "You don't happen to know where we might find it, do you?"

My mind worked furiously to come up with a non-lie. I decided to answer his question with one of my own. "Did she have a safe deposit box?"

"Not that we've been able to determine." He narrowed his eyes. "If—and this is a big if—Kyla was killed because of the manuscript, anyone who had a copy of it might be the next target."

I froze in my seat, then did my best to force my lips into a relaxed smile. "That makes sense. Well, I'm glad you're looking into it."

"I'm still not convinced it was murder, but I'm not going to ignore any leads. I know you and Kyla were friends, and you'd like to find someone to blame, but I'm going to ask you to let me handle the investigation."

"Of course." Although, if he thought I would sit at home twiddling my thumbs while waiting for the results of his half-hearted investigation, he didn't know who he was dealing with. I stood to leave.

"One more thing," he said. "If the toxin was intentionally added to the pickles that were given to you, have you considered that you might have been the intended victim?"

His words stopped me in my tracks. "Why would anyone want to kill me?"

He didn't have an answer, but he did have some advice. "Whoever has a copy of the manuscript may be in danger. If you know anything about the contents of the book, I recommend that you tell no one, not even your friends. I'm the only one in this town you can trust."

JENNIFER'S FATHER stopped by to take her out to dinner. I was happy they'd reconnected. He even tried to be pleasant to me, although it didn't seem to come naturally.

"I guess that means leftovers for me," I said out loud, wondering if Emile would appear in response. Maybe he found watching me heat up leftovers too boring. Or perhaps he considered it beneath him to waste his considerable talents supervising me.

I opened my refrigerator and peered in, but nothing appealed to me. A block of gruyere caught my eye, and I thought, why not? I didn't have to answer to anyone. I could have a grilled cheese sandwich every night of the week if I wanted.

Besides, I'd never tried gruyere in a grilled cheese. Once I'd retrieved the fresh loaf of French bread and grabbed the butter, I pulled down the countertop grill. In no time, I had a gooey, buttery sandwich.

After dinner, I climbed the stairs to my office where my laptop and Kyla's story beckoned me. The clues to her murder had to be there. I began reading the next chapter.

Mayor Green appears on the surface to be the perfect public servant. Someone with her money and resources couldn't possibly be corruptible—or could she?

I skimmed over the next few paragraphs until I got to the interesting and incriminating part:

In need of funds to cover her husband's considerable gambling debts, Mayor Green dipped her sticky fingers into the city coffers, embezzling over a million dollars from Balmy Bay. How did she cover this up? By claiming a budget shortfall and closing all non-essential services, including the beloved library.

Was this true? Did Kyla's story about "Mayor Green" mean that Mayor Gasden had stolen money from the city? I had no idea how to verify or debunk the story, unless I went to Deputy Molina. After all, he'd told me not to trust anyone.

But could I trust him?

CHAPTER 11

I woke up the next morning planning to enjoy the day. I had a feeling it might be my last relaxing Saturday with the grand opening just a week away. I found Jennifer in the kitchen eating a bowl of cereal. Chef Emile was nowhere to be found.

"Do you ever sleep?" I asked.

She grinned in response. "I'm a morning person. I like the quiet, although sometimes the birds can be really loud."

"I'd never noticed." I took the cappuccino she offered. "I think I'll call Irma and invite her over for breakfast, if that's okay with you."

"Of course. But you can probably just put something yummy in the oven and she'll show up. Sometimes I think she can smell you baking from her house."

I laughed. "I think I'll give her a call just to make sure."

When I told Irma I'd decided to try my hand at making chilaquiles, she offered to bring some of her homemade salsa, and I enthusiastically agreed. She arrived to find me frying the last of the tortilla wedges.

"Here you go." She handed me a tub of salsa which I

eagerly opened, dipping a tortilla chip in for a taste. She scolded me. "That's for the chilaquiles."

I grinned. "I thought I'd better taste it first. It's delicious."

Irma scowled. "Of course, it is."

Irma and Jennifer took their seats around the kitchen island while I cooked. I bided my time before springing my questions on Irma, making small talk as I handed each of them their breakfast plates. I took the lack of conversation as a sign they enjoyed their breakfast.

Irma pushed her empty plate away. "Not bad for a gringa."

"Thanks," I said. "That's high praise coming from you."

"Gringa?" Jennifer asked.

"She means non-Latina." I turned to Irma. "Right?"

"Close enough."

"Speaking of close," I said, making an awkward segue to the topic I wanted to broach. "What do you know about Deputy Molina?"

"A little young for you, isn't he?" Irma quipped.

I sighed. "Can you just answer the question for once?"

She snickered, enjoying annoying me as usual. "I'll try. Molina's the acting police chief on a temporary basis, I believe. No one seems to know how long he'll be here."

"Does he live in town?" I asked.

"I think he's staying in Somerton and commuting in. The traffic's not bad right now, but once the summer crowds start arriving, he may regret living twenty miles away." Irma narrowed her eyes at me, an expression I recognized, though I wasn't completely sure what it meant. "Why the interest in Molina?"

"I'm wondering if he can be trusted."

At this, her eyes widened. "I should hope so. Why are you asking?" She eyed me suspiciously. "If we can't trust our police..." She seemed to change her mind mid-sentence, probably in light of recent events. "I'd like to believe our previous chief of police was an aberration."

"What about the mayor?" I knew Irma wasn't fond of Wanda Gasden.

Irma scowled. "What about her?" Irma asked.

Jennifer gasped. "You think she killed Kyla? But she just had a baby."

Irma rolled her eyes. "New mothers are some of the most dangerous creatures ever imagined. They would easily murder to protect their young, even from a perceived threat. Don't you ever watch the National Geographic channel?"

"You think she might be our murderer?" I asked Irma.

"What's her motive?"

"Hiding a secret," I said, not wanting to go into the details. I wasn't ready to tell them I had a copy of Kyla's manuscript. Not yet.

"Everyone has secrets," Irma said. "Even you, I bet."

I glanced over at Chef Emile who said, "She has a point, you must admit."

I gave Irma my best innocent look. "Nothing I'd murder someone for."

CHAPTER 12

*A*fter Irma left, I cleaned up from breakfast while Jennifer got ready to meet a friend for lunch and shopping.

I stared at my cell phone, still not sure I should trust Deputy Molina, but finally decided I didn't have a choice. I had to ask someone about the mayor.

"I hope I'm not disturbing you on a Saturday," I said.

"What's is it?"

"I remembered something else Kyla told me."

"Is that so?" His voice sounded dubious, and I began to doubt if I was fooling him.

"Um, yeah." I took a deep breath and dove in. "She said she had some dirt on the mayor that she planned to include in her novel, changing the names of course so she wouldn't get sued."

"When did she tell you this?" the deputy asked. "The night of the party?"

"I'm not sure."

"Did she share with you the specifics of this dirt she claimed to have?" he asked.

"I think she planned to write that the mayor had embezzled funds and that contributed to the budget shortfall that forced the closing of the library," I said, summarizing what Kyla had written.

"I see." He tapped his pen on the desk. "That was before Mayor Gasden's incumbency. Mayor Gould was running the city back then. Running it into the ground if you ask me."

"Oh." I thanked him for the information and hung up. What a disappointing conversation. All that I'd accomplished was tying my stomach into a knot. I hated lying, but if I told him I had the manuscript, he'd want to see it, and I had to protect my friend.

I didn't want Irma going to jail for an impulsive act years earlier. If she'd pushed Norma down the stairs, I couldn't believe she meant to kill her.

An idea popped into my head. I could delete the part of Kyla's manuscript that implicated Irma and then hand it over to Molina.

Brilliant!

But before I did that, I'd better check and make sure there wasn't anything incriminating any of my other friends. I chuckled to myself. What sort of secrets could Jennifer or Freddie be hiding?

Still, I'd better double check just to make sure.

After Jennifer and I had an early dinner of potato leek soup, I made an excuse to go upstairs so I could continue reading Kyla's manuscript. I'd just opened the file on my laptop when I heard Jennifer calling for me.

When I got halfway down the stairs, I stopped. Sebastian stood just inside the front door looking up at me with a warm smile. Butterflies in my stomach fluttered with approval.

"I hope you don't mind me stopping by," he said. "I had business in the city all day, and on the way back, I couldn't help but think it would be the perfect evening to put the top down and go for a drive. I hoped you would join me."

A ride in a convertible sounded heavenly. I grinned. "I'll just be a minute." I hurried upstairs, pulled my hair into a ponytail, and grabbed a jacket.

We stepped outside and I gazed in surprise at the blue skies, bright sun, and wispy clouds floating leisurely by.

"What happened to June gloom?" I asked as I climbed into the passenger seat.

"I asked Mother Nature for a one-day reprieve, and she agreed," he said, playfully. "Turns out she's quite a romantic."

"Is that so?" If Mother Nature could be charmed, Sebastian would be the man to do it.

We pulled away from my house and Sebastian headed inland. In Serenity Cove, the coastline stretched a mere three miles before being blocked by rocky cliffs at both ends. It was not designed for long coastal drives.

When we reached Shoreline Highway, Sebastian put the top down and headed north along the ocean. I gazed at the waves, gentler than in Serenity Cove. I'd always wondered why our part of the ocean seemed so wild and untamed, but that was one of my favorite things about it.

"I'd love to know more about you," he said. "Come to think of it, I know almost nothing. Where did you grow up?"

"All over the place." With the wind whipping stray strands of hair against my face, I told him the bare minimum about my loving yet unstable mother and absent father, and my unconventional upbringing. "We even spent some time in a commune."

He glanced at me with raised eyebrows. "A commune? What was that like?"

"I was pretty young, like seven or eight, when we first arrived. I barely saw my mother for two years, but that was okay because it was like I had five mothers. They taught me how to bake and make preserves, macrame, all kinds of crafty stuff."

He raised one eyebrow. "Macrame?"

I laughed. "What I loved most was baking. I spent most of my time in the kitchen learning how to make cakes and cookies."

"I guess that explains why you opened a tearoom."

"My mother and I talked about it for years. But after the way I'd been raised, I guess I craved stability, so I got a degree in computer science. I had a great career. I even started up a company with my fiancé—ex-fiancé," I corrected myself. I took a deep breath and hurried to finish that part of my story. "After it went public, we broke up, so I left the company and sold all my shares. Then my mother passed away earlier this year…" I let my voice trail off. The memory of holding her hand for the last time was still so fresh.

He pulled off the road where a rocky cliff overlooked a pebble-strewn beach. "You've been through a lot lately." He turned to face me. "Now you've lost a friend, too. Kyla Bradley was much too young to die." He gazed into my eyes, helping me to forget the past.

I turned away, not wanting to expose my vulnerabilities. "Too young and too talented."

"That's right. Not only a journalist, but also an author, from what I've heard. Did she tell you about the book she was writing?"

"She said it would make a bunch of people unhappy." I tried to remember her exact words. "She said, 'I'd rather be a success than everyone's friend.'"

"An interesting philosophy." He stared out at the ocean. "I wonder where her manuscript is now."

Did everyone in Serenity Cove wonder the same thing? Was he curious like the others, or did he have another reason for asking? Not ready to tell anyone I had a copy, I said, "Me too."

"It's much too rocky here for a walk. I know a better place." He pulled back onto the road. We drove in silence, while I wondered if he'd sensed I'd lied to him. I wanted to tell him the truth, but for now, the fewer people who knew I had Kyla's manuscript, the better. So far, I hadn't told a soul, but I felt the need to confide in someone, to ask for help to understand the clues that I believed it held.

He cleared his throat. "What brought you to Serenity Cove?"

His words brought me out of my reverie. "Fate, serendipity, or luck, I don't know, and guess I don't really need to know." I sighed, thinking of how lucky I'd been to finally find where I belonged. "It feels like home."

"I know what you mean," he said. "San Francisco has never felt that way for me, but it's where I need to be for business. I'm starting to rethink that. It's so much easier to work from wherever you are these days. I miss my old hometown, although a lot has changed. Some of it for the better."

I smiled at the thought that he might move back, especially if his motivation might have something to do with me. "What was it like growing up in Serenity Cove?"

He shot me a grin. "It was torture. I didn't get away with anything. You talk about having five mothers, but I felt like I had a hundred. Any trouble I got into, my mother heard about it before I even got back home."

I suppressed a smile but felt the corners of my mouth turning up. "For a young boy, I can see how that might have been frustrating."

"You have no idea." He kept his eyes on the road, seemingly lost in thought, and I wondered what other memories haunted him.

"Was it hard growing up without a father?" When I didn't get an immediate response, I added, "You don't have to talk about it if you don't want to."

He pulled over to the side of the road and parked the car. "I haven't talked about my childhood in years, but I feel as if I could talk to you about anything." He smiled and took my hand, and I felt my insides turn to mush.

"Uh huh." I glanced out the window to avoid getting lost in his brown eyes. "Did you ever go to the French restaurant at my house when Norma ran it?"

"My mother took me a few times when I was a teenager. That would have been back in the eighties. It was quite wonderful, and Norma was a vision." He gave me a half smile. "I had an enormous crush on her, even though she was nearly my mother's age."

"I've heard she was beautiful." My curiosity compelled me to ask another question. "Did you ever meet the chef that worked there? I believe his name was Emile Toussaint. I have a couple of his cookbooks."

"No, but I heard rumors, of course, especially after he disappeared at the same time that Mrs. Skillings did. I remember my mother saying he could be quite temperamental."

"He is," I said, absentmindedly. "I mean, I heard that too."

"She said he had quite a temper." He smiled. "Enough about the past. I'm more interested in the present. Shall we take a walk?"

We walked to the edge of the cliff, and I looked down at the rocky slope. Hoping he didn't plan for us to scale down it, I felt relief at the sight of concrete stairs. At the bottom, I slipped out of my shoes and let my feet sink into the cool sand. He took my hand and led me along the edge of the water where gentle waves lapped the shore.

Walking along the damp, hard sand, dodging waves, we chatted about everything and nothing while the sun sank lower in the sky. I wished I could stop it from setting so I could stay there on the beach with Sebastian. It felt so natural and comfortable, while at the same time exciting. I'd never had someone as handsome and charming interested in me, but then I'd spent most of my adult years behind a computer screen, hardly ever looking up to see who and what might be out there.

We found a flat rock just large enough for both of us to sit and watch the sun set. The sky turned every shade of pink, orange, and violet before sinking below the horizon.

"I guess that means it's time to go," I said, and we climbed back up the steps to the road. Sebastian pulled the car into my driveway just as a full moon rose above, casting its light on the ocean. I looked over my shoulder at its reflection in the rippling water.

"Beautiful." He spoke softly, as if not wanting to break the spell of the moment.

I turned back to him to find him staring not at the moon but into my eyes.

CHAPTER 13

I might have forgotten to breathe, because I suddenly sucked air into my lungs.

"Are you okay?" he asked.

"Better than okay." I hated to spoil the mood, but I had one question I wanted to ask him before I said goodnight. "Did you know Kyla?"

He flinched ever so slightly, apparently surprised by my question. "I'd seen her on the news a few times. I know she was at your party, but I didn't get a chance to meet her." He took my hand and squeezed it gently. "You're lucky you didn't eat more of the peppers."

"Yes, very lucky." Sebastian seemed to know a lot about what happened at my party, considering he'd only stayed for a brief time. Apparently, Freddie and Molina had managed to keep the true details quiet. In a small town like ours, in the absence of real news, gossip took its place, traveling at lightning speed.

"Did Kyla tell you how far she'd gotten in her writing?" he asked. "Was her book nearly complete?"

"I don't know." I tried to make my expression blank to

80

avoid giving anything away. "Kyla didn't tell me how it was progressing."

"I guess we may never know," he said. "Still, such an unfortunate accident for someone so young. How are you handling the loss?"

"The grand opening has kept me busy, so I haven't dwelled on it too much. I suppose that's a blessing."

"That's right. And I suppose we'll need to get together again to go over my duties as master of ceremonies."

"How about dinner tomorrow?" I suggested. "This time I'll cook."

His smile returned. "That sounds lovely."

He walked me to the front door, and before I could invite him in, he leaned forward and gave me a gentle kiss.

"Goodnight, sweet lady." He returned to his car and drove off.

I hoped Jennifer had gone to her room, because I didn't want to speak to anyone right away. Quietly, I tiptoed into the kitchen to make a cup of chamomile tea.

Chef stood in the middle of the room with his arms crossed over his chest. "And where have you been all evening?"

I nearly told him it was none of his business. "I went for a drive with Sebastian in his convertible. We had a lovely evening and a long talk."

"What do you know about this man?" Chef asked. He dropped his arms and paced from one end of the kitchen to the other while I brewed my tea. He finally said what was on his mind. "I don't trust him."

"Why Emile, are you jealous?" I teased. When he answered with a scowl, I felt a jolt of wonder. Had I struck a nerve?

"Don't be ridiculous. All I am saying is watch your step. Do you hear me?" He looked me in the eye and repeated his warning. "Watch your step." He shimmered briefly before disappearing.

"Well, that was interesting." I stared at the spot where he'd stood moments before. Chef had no one to talk to other than me. For all I knew, he'd been alone for years, unable to communicate. He must have been terribly lonely. And now a man came along who might take me away from him, the only person he had to keep him company and boss around the way he did when he was alive. No wonder he wasn't happy about my new relationship.

I took my tea and climbed the stairs to the second-floor parlor. After pulling a chair over to the window, I watched the moon drop below the horizon.

Happiness felt within reach, and all my cares and worries so far away. But my mind wouldn't allow me to forget about Kyla's death for long. I wouldn't be able to get to sleep after such a wonderful evening, especially not with Kyla's manuscript waiting for me.

I opened my laptop and skimmed forward through several stories and descriptions of people I couldn't connect to anyone I knew. Then, I saw the word "Doctor," and began reading slowly.

I felt my heart sink as I read Kyla's words. They must be lies. It wasn't possible that our wonderful, kind, and ethical Dr. Freddie Severs could have taken someone's life.

CHAPTER 14

*J*ennifer looked up from the island and greeted me with a cheerful, "Good morning!"

"Coffee," I grumbled. After a strong dose of caffeine, I'd decide whether the morning was indeed good or not.

"Up late?"

Jennifer had grown to know me well in a relatively short time. She hopped off her stool and flipped switches on the cappuccino machine.

I reached for one of Emile's cookbooks and paged through hoping a wonderfully intriguing recipe would catch my eye. My ghost chef didn't appear, much to my surprise.

I hoped to impress Sebastian with my French cooking. While I agreed with him that fancy sauces or complicated techniques weren't needed to make wonderful, delicious meals, there was something about a perfectly prepared hollandaise poured over thin spears of asparagus or a poached chicken with a velouté sauce.

"Your phone is buzzing." Jennifer handed me the cappuccino she'd just made, then picked up my phone from the counter, handing it to me.

I stared at the display and frowned. "Sebastian just cancelled." When I got a questioning look in response, I explained that I'd planned to make dinner for him that evening.

"Hmph," came Chef's voice behind me.

I resisted the urge to turn around, since I could imagine his expression.

"Oh, that's too bad he had to cancel." Jennifer perched on a stool across from me.

"What excuse did *ton ament garçon* offer you?" Chef asked. When I didn't reply, he added, "Most bachelors do not find themselves with other responsibilities on a Sunday."

"He has to work," I said, mostly for Chef's benefit. I knew that garçon was French for boy, which was insulting enough, but I'd have to wait to translate the entire phrase he used. I had no doubt I'd find out it meant something derogatory like gigolo or playboy.

"On a Sunday?" Jennifer asked while Chef gave a huff to show his disbelief.

"I'm working today, aren't I?" My annoyance at Chef must have seeped into my voice, based on Jennifer's reaction.

"Sorry," she said.

"No, I'm sorry. I'm just a little cranky because I stayed up too late reading and there's a lot to do before the grand opening."

"What should we do first?" Jennifer jumped up from her stool ready to get to work.

"How about I make us some breakfast?" Maybe food would improve my mood. "I'm thinking Toad in the Hole."

"Toad?" she scrunched her face trying to make sense of what I'd said. "I'm still getting used to the idea of eating snails."

I laughed. "No toads will be harmed in the making of our breakfast. The classic Toad in the Hole is made from sausages in Yorkshire pudding batter, but I'm making the American version—toast with a fried egg in the middle. It's easy and quick."

"Easy enough that I could make it?" She'd always been insecure about her cooking skills having been raised by a father who didn't cook.

"I'll show you how," I said. "In fact, why don't you make it and I'll walk you through how I do it."

She grinned. "You may regret that decision."

WE SURVIVED THE COOKING LESSON, and Jennifer even offered to clean up the breakfast dishes. I took my cup of tea and my task list for the fundraiser to the front room. The marine layer hung over the ocean stubbornly, but I hoped the sun would make an appearance by early afternoon.

My phone buzzed again, this time with a text from Deputy Molina asking to see me. Oddly, he asked me to meet him in Hiverton and suggested that I not tell anyone. I told Jennifer I had some errands to run and hopped into my car for the thirty-minute drive.

Hiverton, about twenty miles inland from Serenity Cove, had all the amenities we didn't and none of the charm. I drove down the main road, lined with spindly trees. Dead leaves collected in the gutter and brown lawns fronted dull-looking homes. A brown haze hung over the town.

When I pulled up to the address Molina had texted, I hesitated before getting out of the car. Reading his text again, I confirmed this was the place.

A fading sign had been painted on the brick building: Bub's Bar and Grill. If Molina didn't want anyone from

Serenity Cove to run into us, he'd picked the right place. I locked my car and hoped I'd find him inside waiting for me.

The moment the door closed behind me, I blinked repeatedly, unable to see anything in the dim light. I heard my name, grateful when the deputy came to my rescue and led me to a booth.

I slid into the worn, brown-upholstered seat, noting the duct tape patches. "Nice place," I said, not trying to hide my sarcasm. "What's going on?"

He chuckled. "I guess this isn't the sort of place you normally frequent."

"You do?" My eyes began to adjust to the lack of light. The decor was just what I expected, with sticky, wood-grained Formica tables and linoleum floors. Relieved to see that the few patrons didn't appear to be ax murderers, I relaxed.

"I always come here when I don't want to be seen. Or overheard. I've never run into anyone I know."

"No surprise there. Why all the secrecy?"

He leaned back in the booth and didn't answer right away. "This case has me stumped. And I honestly don't know who I can trust."

The bartender came over and asked if we wanted something. I would have loved a mimosa, but it didn't seem like the place for it. Molina ordered us two draft beers. We sat quietly in the dark waiting for our beers while I wondered about Molina's agenda.

When our non-frosty mugs arrived, I broke the silence. "If you can't trust anyone, why am I here?"

"You've been in Serenity Cove, what? Two months?" When I nodded, he continued. "You're still an outsider in this town."

That stung a bit. I'd felt like an outsider my entire life. Serenity Cove felt like home to me, and I'd made a few friends. But he was right. I had yet to win over most of the locals.

He took a long sip of his beer before telling me why he'd asked me to meet him. "I've talked to Dr. Severs, and she's convinced the poisoning was intentional, and that Kyla was the intended victim, not you." He paused. "I'm guessing you knew that already."

"I figured as much." I waited to hear what else he had to say.

"Kyla didn't have any enemies—no stalker or jealous ex-boyfriend. My only theory is that someone didn't want the book she was writing to see the light of day. That means that everyone in town is potentially a suspect, at least until I can locate her manuscript and find out whose secrets she's written into her story." He paused. "You're the only person I'm sure she didn't write into her book."

"Because I'm new in town."

He nodded, taking another long drink of his beer. "And that's why you should trust me too. I'm not from Serenity Cove."

He had a point. I, like him, didn't know who I could trust. But I wasn't ready to turn over the manuscript to him until I knew what secrets it contained.

I took a sip of my beer to stall for time. He might not be a suspect, but I had no idea what his loyalties were. For one thing, he worked closely with the mayor, and she might not have murdered Kyla, but I didn't trust her.

"So where do we go from here?" I asked.

"I'd really like to see Kyla's manuscript," he said, getting right to the point.

I smiled, hoping it didn't appear as fake as it felt. "Me too. Do you know who has it?"

He leaned back in the booth, tilting his head as if sizing

me up. "Oh, so that's how it's going to be. So much for trusting me. I can get a search warrant, you know."

"If I had the manuscript, which I'm not saying I do, that would be an empty threat. I worked in computer science for years. I know how to erase a file so it can never be retrieved." I took another sip of beer to give me time to gather my thoughts, then remembered I didn't really like beer. "If I had it—"

"Which you're not saying you do," he said, finishing my sentence.

I smiled, happy we were starting to understand each other. "If I did have it, I might want another couple of days to look into the incriminating information it might contain about one or two of my friends."

He leaned forward, his elbows on the table. "Like what, for instance?"

"Let's say Norma Thornly's death might not have been an accident, and maybe someone pushed her down the stairs."

"Norma Thornly?" He gave me a quizzical look. "The woman who once ran a French restaurant in your house? But that was decades ago, everyone from back then is—" His eyes widened. "Oh. Not all of them are dead."

"I'm not letting someone go to jail for something that happened that long ago."

He stared into his beer as if it had an answer for him. "Anyone who'd been alive then would be pretty old now. They might die in jail."

"Exactly."

He brightened up. "I can look into Norma's death and see if there's any truth to Kyla's story." He wrote himself a note. "I'll see if I can dig up the police report. I hope it's been put in digital format. Otherwise, I'll have to spend some time digging through the storeroom and going through a bunch of dusty old files." He gave me a serious look. "If the records show the story is fabricated, which I suspect it is, then will you turn the manuscript over to me?" When I didn't answer, he rephrased his question. "Or should I say, *if* you had the manuscript?"

"There's more." I had his full attention now. "Dr. Severs—not Freddie, but her father, passed away a few years ago after a long illness."

"Go on," he prompted.

"There's a rumor that his death wasn't a hundred percent due to natural causes—that it was, well, sped up."

"And, in the story, is it the doctor's daughter who helps speed up his death?"

I took a deep breath. "If someone hastened his death, they might have believed it was out of kindness, to end his suffering."

Molina gave me a firm stare. "It's still murder."

I stared at him, angry at both him and myself. I slid out of the booth. "I shouldn't have told you. You said I could trust you, but I never should have believed you."

I heard him call after me as I headed for the door, but I just kept walking. I'd never forgive myself if Freddie got arrested all because I couldn't keep a secret.

CHAPTER 15

Sleeping in late was becoming a habit after years of rising at the crack of dawn. The sound of footsteps coming up the stairs caught my attention and I hurried to finish dressing. I opened my door to see if Jennifer needed me for something.

"Someone's here to see you," she said in a sing-song voice.

I slipped into my shoes and came downstairs where Deputy Molina stood in the front room. He looked out of place among the tables covered in flowery tablecloths. I scowled at him, still angry. But was I angry at him or myself?

He said nothing until I reached the bottom step. "I just wanted to tell you what I learned in person."

I motioned for him to take a seat by the bay window and sat down across from him. "Okay. Tell me."

He looked uncomfortable, but what sort of reception did he expect after practically saying he'd arrest my friend for murder?

"After we met yesterday, I dug up the police report for the investigation into Norma's death. Apparently, her sister

Barbara had accused Irma of pushing Norma down the stairs."

My heart began beating faster. "Great," I said, my voice oozing sarcasm. "Do you have any more good news for me?"

He gave me a wry smile. "The file contains about a dozen witness reports from people who said Irma was at the Mermaid Cafe at the time Norma fell. She wasn't responsible for Norma's death."

I felt my breathing return to normal. "I didn't for a moment think Irma could murder someone, but I was afraid they'd had a fight and she'd shoved Norma. Apparently, there was a lot of bad blood between them."

Molina smiled. "Does this mean you're willing to trust me?"

"No," I blurted out. I lowered my voice. "What about Freddie? Are you going to pursue a case against her?"

Molina shook his head. "Freddie is a well-respected doctor with impeccable ethical standards. I don't believe for a moment she had anything to do with her father's death."

"Me neither." But if the story got out, it could damage Freddie's reputation.

"It seems obvious to me that Kyla took a bunch of old, unsubstantiated rumors and innuendo and turned it into some kind of melodramatic trash." He stood up to go. "I doubt that anything in that book has any basis in reality."

"Then why was she killed?" I asked, walking him to the door.

He turned back to me. "Have you considered it might have nothing to do with the book?"

It hadn't occurred to me. "Why else would someone murder Kyla?" As far as I knew, the only enemies she had were ones she'd made while researching her novel. "Maybe someone has a secret and was afraid she'd discovered the truth. It's possible she didn't even write about it."

"Maybe she used the information to blackmail someone," he said.

"Blackmail?" His remark caught me by surprise. Would Kyla be willing to blackmail someone? I knew how ambitious she'd been and how eagerly she wanted to move to a big city and make a name for herself. I had no idea what lengths she might have gone to in search of success.

"It's just a thought." Molina stepped onto the porch, turning back to get one last word in. "But don't worry. I'll find out who murdered Kyla."

I stood by the front door while he walked to his patrol car. He couldn't be more than thirty years old. What did he know about solving a murder?

I waited for Irma to stop by to mooch lunch or a mid-afternoon snack, but she didn't show. I gave her a call, and she suggested I stop by the Mermaid Café.

"I keep the front door locked until opening time, so come around the side door," she instructed.

I stepped outside, and the bright sunshine surprised me. I went back inside for sunglasses, which took me twenty minutes to find. I hadn't needed them since I'd moved to Serenity Cove with the constant overcast and relentless drizzle. I walked along the beach path, enjoying the sunshine and the sight of the sparkling, blue water until I came to the pier and the ramshackle wooden building that housed Irma's restaurant.

I stepped through the side door into the dark interior and called out, "Irma?"

"Over here," she called out from the far end of the bar. I found her sitting on a barstool polishing glasses. She handed me a towel. "Here. You can help. I hate hard water spots."

I perched on a stool and grabbed a glass, talking as I wiped. "I have a confession to make. But you can't tell anyone." I waited for a response, but she only raised her eyebrows at me, so I continued. "I have a copy of Kyla's book."

"What?" Irma exclaimed, nearly dropping the glass she held.

I nodded. "I've been reading it, but it's been slow going. The prose is stilted and overwritten, so it's taken me some time to get through it. There's a thinly veiled story about you, claiming that you pushed Norma down the stairs. She doesn't use your real name, of course, since it's supposedly fiction, but it's not hard at all to tell who she based the characters on."

Irma's face, impassive at first, darkened until I began to worry.

"I know you didn't do it," I said. "Deputy Molina found the original police report, and—"

"What?" She jumped off her stool and put her hands on her hips like a tiny tyrant. "You talked to Molina before you came to me?"

When she put it that way, it didn't make me look good. "I didn't want to talk to anyone. I wanted to find out who had a motive to kill Kyla." I stopped when I realized I was making it worse. "I didn't want you to be accused of killing Kyla because of some stupid old story. Molina asked me to meet him and, I don't know. I guess he got me to trust him."

Her head bobbed up and down. "I see. You trust him, but you don't trust me."

"It's not that. It's… I don't know." I folded my arms on the bar and lay my head on them. "I need your help."

"Oh, sure. Now that you need my help, you'll tell me everything. Now that you know I'm not a murderer."

I tried to explain that I never thought she'd actually murdered Norma, but that I didn't want the rumor getting out until I knew the whole story.

"I've lived with that rumor for thirty years," she said. "And there've been plenty of others too. I'm done caring what they say about me."

"What about what people say about Freddie?"

Irma climbed back onto her barstool. "If anyone besmirches that girl's name, then I just might resort to murder."

I gave her a quick summary of the story Kyla had written about the fictional doctor and his daughter. "Do you think Freddie might have given him something for the pain and maybe given him too much?"

"No," she said. "She's too good of a doctor. And don't even begin to think she would have done it on purpose, even to end his suffering."

"Okay, I believe you," I said, relieved to let go of my suspicions. "But will everyone else?"

IRMA'S WORDS stayed in my thoughts while I perched on a boulder next to the pier watching the waves crash below. The sun hung low in the sky as clouds began to gather. Why had I not trusted her?

The truth—I didn't trust anyone. In the first fifty years of my life, trusting someone often hadn't gone well. How did people know who to trust and who not to trust? How did they avoid getting hurt?

Maybe it was time to throw caution to the wind and start believing in people. It seemed a more pleasant way to live as long as they didn't end up betraying me. Could I undo all the years I'd spent learning to be a cynic? I felt ready to give it a try, so I stood and headed for home, planning to give Freddie a call as soon as I got there.

When I arrived, her car sat parked in my driveway. Good. Talking to her in person would be even better.

I hurried up the wooden steps impatient to talk with her. The moment I opened the front door, I heard her call my name, and not in a friendly way.

"April May, what business do you have going around making accusations about me?" Freddie wore a professional, navy-blue pantsuit and a grim expression.

My mouth dropped open before it hit me. "Did Irma call you?" I'd asked her not to repeat what I had said. So much for trusting her.

The look in her eyes told me I'd guessed right. "How dare you."

"I didn't accuse you of anything," I explained. "Kyla did. And I planned to give you a call as soon as I got here to tell you everything."

She folded her arms over her chest. "And how long have you had the manuscript? We talked about it the day after Kyla died, and you didn't say a word. Just let me go on and on wondering who might have a copy of it. You must have felt so smug, knowing just where it was and what was on it."

"I only realized I had it after we talked. Kyla had slipped it in the jacket I was wearing." I could tell she didn't believe me. "Look, I might be guilty of not telling you as soon as I realized I had the manuscript, but I'm not lying. I didn't even know what was on the flash drive until I started reading it. The first story was all about the Thornly sisters and claimed that Irma pushed Norma down the stairs. How did I know that didn't happen?"

Freddie's eyes widened. "You thought Irma was a murderer?"

"No, of course not. But don't tell me you couldn't imagine Irma giving someone a good shove if they got on her nerves."

Freddie opened her mouth to speak, then closed it again.

I gave her a tentative smile. "I mean, I wouldn't want to tick her off, would you?"

Freddie's mouth began to twitch, and one corner turned up, a snicker escaping her before she could stop it. She turned away while she composed herself, obviously not ready to stop being angry with me.

Jennifer came halfway down the stairs and watched us for a moment. "What's going on?"

Freddie glanced up at Jennifer, then at me. "I'm still mad at you."

"I understand," I said somberly.

"Why?" Jennifer asked, completely confused by the two of us.

I glanced at Freddie, and she shook her head the tiniest bit, telling Jennifer, "Sometimes you get mad at your friends. It's nothing, really."

"Okay." Jennifer clearly didn't believe her. She headed for the kitchen. "I'll make a fresh pot of peach herbal tea so you can talk over your 'nothing.'"

We took a seat by the bay window, and once we had our tea, Jennifer left us alone to talk. I summarized the story about the doctor and his daughter that Kyla had written.

"So, it was obvious it referred to me and my dad," she said, once I'd finished.

"It sure was." I waited for her to tell me the real version of what had happened to her father, the small-town doctor and county coroner who she'd revered and emulated.

"It's true that he asked me to help end his suffering." She stared at her hands folded in her lap. "I couldn't do it. I'm still not sure if I made the right decision, but I have to live with it."

"You might have lost your license, right?"

She looked up at me and blinked moist eyes. "I told myself it was wrong, that it was against the law." She took a deep breath. "But the truth is, I was selfish."

"Selfish?" That went against everything I knew about her.

She smiled weakly. "I didn't want to let him go. I would have done anything possible to keep him alive. He spent his last weeks on this earth in a hospital on life support. My mother wanted to turn off the respirator, but I couldn't let him go. It's my fault he suffered so much."

Freddie stood and walked toward the window, not wanting me to see her tears. Her sniffles gave her away. I ducked into another room for a box of tissues, and when I returned, she'd gone.

CHAPTER 16

I took a scoop of kibble up to the attic for Whisk. Standing among all the clutter, I called for him, then jumped when he rubbed against the back of my leg.

"Hey, pal, I brought your dinner."

I poured his food into the bowl, and he eyed it before turning his face up to mine as if to say, "That's it? That's what you're going to feed me?"

"I called the vet and that's what he recommended," I explained to the cat as if he could understand me.

Whisk sauntered away, disappearing among all the boxes and furniture. The attic held so many odds and ends along with cartons full of things I didn't know what to do with. Maybe I'd have a yard sale, but not until after the grand opening was out of the way.

But what to do with the papers and documents that had come with the house? One of these days, I'd have to sort through them all to make sure there wasn't anything important before shredding them.

I reached into the box Whisk had been curled up in before. He'd seemed so protective of its contents. *What a silly thought.* I pulled out some of the papers, quickly scanning them. Some looked worthless, like an ad for a dry cleaner and an old newspaper. One of them appeared to be a legal document, a deed, printed on yellowed, fragile paper. The address was 249 Elm Street. I'd passed by Elm but couldn't remember whether the buildings there were businesses or homes.

I dug through the rest of the papers and pulled out a file labeled tax returns. Looking inside, I saw several years from 1958 through 1960. The restaurant had been open during that time, and I took a glance at the income and expenses shown. It would be interesting to see how profitable the restaurant had once been.

Then I recognized something that gave me a thrill. A menu for Maison Rose, the restaurant that had once occupied the first floor of my home. I couldn't wait to show that to my friends. I took the deed and the tax returns to review later when I had some time to kill, though I didn't anticipate that would be anytime soon.

"See you later, Whisk."

The cat reappeared, looking disappointed that I hadn't yet returned with a more suitable dinner. He watched me walk down the attic stairs. I put the deed and tax return in the desk drawer in my office and took the menu downstairs to show Jennifer.

"Hey, check this out." Finding her in the kitchen making a sandwich, I asked, "Is that what you're having for dinner?"

"Yeah, I thought I'd heat up some soup to go with it if that's okay."

"Great idea. I'll join you."

We had enough soup in the walk-in freezer to feed us for months, so I retrieved a frozen block and put it in a saucepan to heat up while I made a grilled cheese sandwich to go with it. Grilled cheese with a bowl of soup was one of my top ten favorite comfort foods.

"What did you want me to check out?" Jennifer asked.

"I found an old menu from when this place was a French restaurant." I stirred the pot and gestured toward the island where I'd left it.

Jennifer picked it up and began reading. "Hors d'oeuvres. Marinated herring. Scampi a la maison. Escargot bourguignonne. Are escargot really snails?"

"They are. They're also delicious."

"Yuck." She grimaced, then kept reading. "Entrees. Coq au vin." She looked up. "Your phone is buzzing again."

She handed me the phone and I checked my messages. One in particular made me smile.

"Good news?" she asked.

"Sebastian asked if I'm free tomorrow night." I typed my response, inviting him over so that I could cook for him as I'd planned to do on Sunday.

"My dad's been bugging me to come over and visit," Jennifer said. "I think I'll do that tomorrow and let you have the house to yourself."

CHEF WATCHED me fry the bacon in the Dutch oven, nagging me not to let it overcook. After removing the bacon, which I set aside, I turned up the heat as his recipe for coq au vin instructed.

"Now, you may sear the chicken until golden brown," he said. "I do not understand why you have chosen chicken pieces without the bone. These pieces are missing the... *je nais se quois.*"

I translated the phrase literally. *"You don't know what? I do."* I laid the pieces in the pan one by one. "They're missing the messy awkwardness of trying to cut a piece of chicken around a bone while everything is dripping in sauce." I glanced at him, always so self-assured. I wished I had his confidence. "I know you get frustrated with my little short-cuts, but I'm not half the chef you are."

He tried to hide his pleasure from my compliment, but failed, clearing his throat instead. "You could excel if you only made a true effort. French cuisine is an art, and I believe you have the soul of an artist."

"Ha!" I turned to face him, expecting to see evidence of him mocking me. Instead, his steel-blue eyes gazed into mine as if trying to express something he couldn't put into words.

"I mean every word I say," he said, reaching out to me.

I held my breath, spellbound as his transparent hand came closer to mine.

Jennifer's voice broke the spell. "My dad's picking me up any minute." She stood in the kitchen doorway. "Are you okay?"

"Of course." I turned back to the stove, pushing the chicken pieces around in the pan. "Have a good time."

"You too." She snickered. "Don't do anything I wouldn't do."

Emile's voice brought me back to the task at hand. "I said sear the chicken, not burn."

I rushed to flip the pieces over, while wondering what had just happened. As crazy as it might seem to take cooking advice from a ghost, it would be even crazier to fall in love with one.

Luckily, I had a real, live man on the way to focus on.

Jennifer answered the door at the same moment I realized I'd forgotten to take my hair out of the ponytail I always wore when I cooked. Maybe it was time for Sebastian to see the "real" me, so I could find out if he was still interested.

Chef scowled at me. The kindly demeanor he'd briefly

demonstrated was nowhere to be found. "That man is here again."

"Behave yourself," I hissed.

Sebastian entered the kitchen and inhaled deeply. "It smells heavenly in here." He gave me a kiss on the cheek and watched over my shoulder as I stirred the red wine sauce.

"Thank you." I ignored Chef's glare and motioned toward the counter. "Would you mind handing me the mushrooms and bacon?"

Chef took a step closer to us. "What about the haricot vert?"

Sebastian slid the mushrooms into the pot, followed by the bacon. I glanced at the colander full of the French green beans I'd rinsed earlier. I'd completely forgotten about them until Chef reminded me.

"Are you planning to cook the haricot vert?" he asked.

"Yes!" I snapped.

Sebastian's eyes widened in surprise.

"I'm so sorry," I covered my mouth, shocked by my own behavior and trying to think how to recover. I could hardly tell him the ghost of a French chef was getting on my nerves. "I get so stressed out when I'm cooking. I'm afraid I forget my manners."

Sebastian gave me an indulgent smile. "Why don't you keep stirring, and I'll cook the green beans. Shall I steam them?"

Chef folded his arms over his chest and smirked. "This man knows nothing about French cuisine. Why do you allow him to assist you?"

I did my best to tune out the ghost's words. "I thought I'd boil them briefly, maybe five minutes, then toss them with sautéed shallots." That's how Emile had taught me.

"Very well," Sebastian said with a warm smile. "You're the

boss." He filled the pot with water and placed it on one of the back burners. "I see you've already chopped the shallots."

"I'm trying to learn to prep the ingredients in advance, the way the cookbook says."

"Ah, yes. Mise en place." Sebastian picked up the old cookbook off the counter. "Is this the cookbook you're using?" He flipped a few pages and laughed. "Such old-fashioned advice."

At this comment, Chef walked right up to Sebastian, scowling at him, nose to nose. Sebastian brushed his face as if he'd felt a tickle.

"Old fashioned, indeed," Chef said. "I suppose this man can teach you how to make modern cuisine. Such as TV dinners."

I suppressed a laugh. "Chef Emile Toussaint may be old fashioned, but he's been the best teacher I've ever had."

Sebastian lowered the fire under the pot, added the green beans, then turned to me. "You talk about him as if he's alive and here in your kitchen with you."

"I almost feel like he is," I admitted, more truthfully than he knew. "Is that weird?"

"I think it's delightful." He reached up and pushed a stray lock of hair behind my ear. "Should I be jealous? I'm not sure how to compete with someone who isn't even real."

I heard a hissing sound and turned to see the pot boiling over. "The beans!"

Sebastian turned the fire down lower. "I'm not doing very well with my one job, am I? If you will stop distracting me with your charming ways…"

"Me? Distracting you?" I laughed. "Maybe next time we should have the food delivered."

When the dish was ready, I ladled servings of coq au vin onto the plates, and Sebastian added a scoop of haricot vert. I proudly regarded the dishes before picking them up to carry into the other room.

"We can eat here at the island," he suggested.

"No!" I blurted out. I glanced at Chef who gave me a smirk. I didn't want to listen to his snide remarks while trying to have a conversation with Sebastian. "We'll be more comfortable in the front room. Would you grab the wine? I've already opened it."

I left my phone buzzing in the kitchen while I carried our meals. I'd set a table by the bay window with a view of the ocean. We still had an hour of daylight ahead, and the streaks of clouds hovering over the ocean promised a stunning sunset.

He didn't talk until he'd taken the last bite of coq au vin. Leaning back in his chair, he said one word. "Delicious."

I grinned. "I'm glad you enjoyed it."

I stood to carry our dishes to the kitchen, refusing his offer of help. "I'll be right back, and we can watch the sunset from the front porch."

My phone buzzed again, and I couldn't resist checking it. Five missed calls from the caterer and three messages. As I listened to the first voicemail message, my heart sank. When I returned to the front room, Sebastian took one look at me and asked me what was wrong.

I reminded myself to breathe. "The caterer. They've cancelled."

"What do you mean cancelled?"

"For the Grand Opening Saturday. *This* Saturday." I counted on my fingers. "Four days from now." I collapsed in my chair and put my face in my hands. "What am I going to do?" I mumbled. "I'll never get another caterer on such short notice."

He patted my shoulder reassuringly. "We can figure it out."

I looked up doubtfully. "We've sold nearly a hundred tickets, and they weren't cheap."

"Of course, they weren't. It's a fundraiser for a good cause. That's what people expect to pay."

"Yes, and they also expect fancy canapés and gourmet hors d'oeuvres served by tuxedoed servers along with their champagne and cocktails. Mini quiches aren't going to cut it."

He took my hands in his and gave them a squeeze. "Let me make a few calls in the morning. I'll stop by in the afternoon and see what we can do."

"No, it's my problem," I said, much more accustomed to taking care of my own problems than letting a man fix things for me.

"Everyone can use help, even a superwoman like you." He leaned over and kissed me on my cheek. "See you tomorrow."

CHAPTER 17

*J*ennifer waited until she set my morning cappuccino in front of me before she began interrogating me. "So... how was dinner?"

"Great," I said. "The coq au vin came out wonderfully. There's leftovers if you want to try some for lunch."

"That's not what I meant, and you know it." Jennifer grabbed a carton from the refrigerator and poured herself a glass of orange juice. "I've already had two mochas," she said. "Even I have my limit."

Three raps on the back door made us turn to each other and say in unison, "Irma."

Irma entered and stopped just inside the door. "What are you two looking at?"

"Nothing," we both said at once, then laughed.

Irma put her hands on her hips. "I don't know what's gotten into you two." She pulled up a stool. "How'd the date go?"

"Apparently," Jennifer said, "the coq au vin was delicious."

"Not the information I was looking for," Irma said. "Come on, April. Give us the good stuff."

106

I sighed. "Not much to tell. As soon as I found out the caterer had cancelled—"

Jennifer stopped what she was doing. "They cancelled?"

"But the grand opening is Saturday." Irma took a seat on a stool across from me. "What are we going to do?"

I looked from Jennifer to Irma and back again. "We?"

"Of course," Irma said. "What did you think?"

I grinned. I liked being part of a "we."

Irma, Jennifer, and I spent the rest of the morning brainstorming, coming up with appetizers that looked and tasted fancy without taking too much time and effort. Irma and I flipped through Emile's cookbooks while Jennifer checked online recipes on her phone.

"Blinis with creme fraiche and caviar?" Irma suggested.

"Yum," Jennifer said, then gave me a half smile. "What are blinis?"

"Little pancakes," I explained. "That sounds perfect. Also, delicious and fancy." Just the sort of appetizer I needed to impress my guests. "And not too much work. I can make the blinis ahead of time and put the toppings on the night of the party."

"You have to make your cheese puffs." Irma said. She'd been bugging me to make them again since I'd served them at my open house several weeks earlier.

"That can be arranged." I'd already decided to make them part of the evening's menu. "How about crostini? I can make the toast that morning and make a variety of toppings." I scanned the possible combinations in the cookbook. "Roasted cherry tomatoes, burrata, and basil pesto sounds wonderful."

Jennifer read over my shoulder. "Mmm... Prosciutto, manchego cheese, and fig jam. What's manchego cheese?"

"Expensive, I'm guessing," Irma said.

"Who's up for a trip to San Francisco?" Most of the ingredients we needed wouldn't be found in Serenity Cove, or even in the larger town of Somerton, twenty miles away.

"Me, me, me!" Jennifer jumped up and down with excitement.

"You two have fun on your shopping expedition." Irma got up from her stool and threw her purse over her shoulder. "While you're gone, I'll ask the Friends of the Library if they've got a volunteer or two to act as servers for the evening. I'll pay for the tuxedo rentals," she said, adding, "It's tax deductible."

Before Irma managed to slip out the back door, the doorbell rang. I found Sebastian at the front door and returned with him to the kitchen. He'd known Irma since he was a child growing up in town. She gave him a less-than-warm greeting, but that was pretty much normal for Irma.

He gave me a peck on the cheek, which brought raised eyebrows from my friends, then handed me a printout of a menu from a high-end San Francisco restaurant.

"I'm friends with the owner," he said. "They can take care of all the catering. Just order what you want, and it will be delivered Saturday in time for the event."

I jumped off the stool and gave him a hug, which maybe went on longer than necessary. When I let him go, I said, "Thank you so much, but I think I'm going to make the appetizers. With Jennifer's help." I felt a twinge of guilt after he'd gone to the trouble of finding a restaurant to cater my event. "Not that I don't appreciate your help. I don't want you to think I'm ungrateful."

"Not at all." Sebastian gave me a concerned look. "But are you sure? It's going to be a lot of work."

"You know I love to cook, and what better way to showcase our tearoom than providing the food ourselves? We might book some future events if people like what they see."

"And taste," Irma added.

"If that's what you want," he said, sounding a little disappointed. "Tell you what. I'll contribute a couple of cases of champagne. That should give you one less thing to think about."

"Really?" I jumped up and gave him another hug, but just a quick one this time. "Thank you!"

"I'll let you and your friends get back to work." He gave me another kiss on the cheek. "I'll let myself out. Call me if you need anything else."

After he left, Irma said, "I can think of one or two things you might need from that man."

I swatted her on the arm. "I thought you were leaving."

She headed for the back door, mumbling, "I can tell when I'm not wanted."

THURSDAY, Jennifer and I made the drive to San Francisco, visiting three grocery stores to get all the exotic ingredients we needed.

When we returned and put all our purchases away, I reviewed the list of appetizers and desserts to determine what could be done in advance. The first recipe on the list, blinis with creme fraiche and caviar, would have to be assembled on Saturday, but the blinis could be made ahead of time and frozen. On Saturday, all I needed to do was heat them up in the oven for a few minutes.

"What can I do?" Jennifer asked as I reached in the refrigerator and pulled out the last stick of butter.

I searched behind the milk and in all the drawers, unable to accept that I'd left such an important item off my grocery list. "We're out of butter."

"I'll run to the store," Jennifer volunteered. "Anything else we need?"

We checked the other staples, adding a few more items to the list.

After sending Jennifer off to the store, I mixed the batter for the blinis. I got out my largest skillet, tossed a pat of butter in the pan, and waited for it to melt. As I was about to begin, Chef appeared, startling me.

"Can you give me a warning when you're about to materialize?" I grumbled. "Like a 'psst' or something?"

"Place a few drops of water in the pan," Chef suggested. "If they skitter, it is ready."

"Skitter?" I asked. "Is that a technical term?" He ignored my comment, so I gave it a try. The water drops sizzled slightly but didn't move. "So... not ready?"

He sighed dramatically. "What do you think?"

I waited another minute and tried again. The drop of water danced across the pan just as he'd said it would.

I poured the batter into the pan, one tablespoon at a time, making perfectly round pancakes.

Emile looked over my shoulder. "Now you wait for the bubbles."

I watched until a few appeared. "Ooh! Bubbles! Do I flip them now?"

"Wait for the bubbles to pop and when they make little holes in the top, then you may turn them."

As much as Emile's criticism bugged me at times, I loved having him in the kitchen to help me follow his complicated recipes and teaching me insider tips. I'd learned so much from him in a relatively short time.

I'd removed the last batch of blinis to a platter and covered them when Jennifer returned.

"Can I try one?" she asked.

I held out the plate for her, and she inhaled the blini in two bites. "Hungry?" I asked.

She gave me a sheepish look. "I forgot to eat lunch."

"Me too." I remembered the leftovers. "How about sharing what's left of last night's coq au vin?"

I reheated our lunch, and we ate while going over the tasks that remained to get ready for the fundraiser.

"What about drinks?" she asked. "Have you thought about it?"

"Sebastian is donating the champagne." A memory of a cocktail I'd seen once in a magazine popped into my head. "We could offer something fancier. With tea." I jumped up out of my chair and retrieved a plastic pouch.

Jennifer gave me a quizzical look as she read the label on the packet. "Butterfly pea flower tea?"

I refilled the electric kettle and flipped the switch. While I waited for the water to boil, I found two glass teacups. This was the perfect time to use them.

I brewed the tea, then poured it into the cups. It was a beautiful, vibrant shade of blue.

"Wow!" Jennifer exclaimed. "How pretty!" She took a sip. "It tastes nothing like I expected."

"It's a surprisingly mild taste." I took a sip of my tea then put it in the freezer. I retrieved a bottle of sparkling wine in the refrigerator and set it on the island along with a squeeze bottle of simple syrup and a lemon.

Jennifer grinned. "Champagne so early in the day? What are we celebrating?"

I popped open the bottle, grabbed a couple of flutes, then retrieved my not-quite-so-hot tea. I poured some tea and simple syrup into the first glass then filled it to the top with sparkling wine.

"What a great idea," Jennifer said. "Hey, it's turning purple."

"Oh." The color change surprised me too, but for a different reason. "It wasn't supposed to do that until I added the lemon. I guess the acid in the champagne did it."

I added a squeeze of lemon anyway for an extra bit of flavor.

Jennifer clapped her hands. "That's going to be the hit of the party."

Appreciating Jennifer's enthusiasm, I regarded the drink, then took a sip. "It tastes good too." I let her have a sip and she agreed. "Now, let's try a non-alcoholic version."

I repeated the steps, substituting sparkling water for the champagne. This time, the bright blue drink didn't turn purple until I added lemon juice. I let Jennifer take the first taste.

"I like it," she said. "And how fun to have a pretty cocktail like this for people who don't drink."

"And for us. We'll want to stay sober at least until the guests leave. And then we'll probably be exhausted and go straight to bed. I'm sure I will."

CHAPTER 18

Friday flew by with all the last-minute preparations. Jennifer had brought down all the old books from the attic, and after dusting them, displayed them in the former bedroom I'd decided to turn into a sort of library. We'd moved half of the tables to the garage to make room for everyone, arranging some of the chairs along the walls to give the attendees places to sit. This left a roomy open area for people to mingle.

We'd cleaned and scrubbed every inch of the first story, polished the tile floors until they gleamed, and shined every crystal on the two enormous chandeliers.

When Saturday morning arrived at long last, I jumped out of bed before the alarm went off. After a quick shower, I put on some comfy, casual clothes since I'd be spending the morning in the kitchen preparing appetizers.

The six high-fashion mannequins we'd ordered arrived, and I called Irma so she could bring over the vintage designer dresses and gowns we'd be displaying. She stopped by to pick up Jennifer, and they went together to retrieve the garments she'd had in storage for decades.

When they returned, Jennifer honked her horn as a signal for me to come help. We carried in ten boxes which had been professionally cleaned and boxed decades earlier. I'd been bugging Irma for days to bring the dresses over so we could make sure they were still in presentable condition.

Jennifer and I watched expectantly as she opened the first box.

"This is a Balenciaga," Irma said, lifting a vibrant, red long-sleeved dress from its container. It had a cinched waist and full skirt. On me, it would have fallen mid-calf, but on Irma, it must have come down to her ankles. She laid it carefully on one of the tables, then moved on to the next.

As she held up a white jacket with a peplum waist, Jennifer gasped. "That's Dior!" She took a step closer and leaned in, as if drawn to the garment yet afraid to get too close. "Dior's new look," she repeated, turning to me. "From the late forties." She seemed disappointed in my lack of understanding. She turned back to Irma, excited. "This should be in a museum."

Irma scoffed. "They can have them when I'm dead." She lifted the full, black skirt that paired with the jacket. "Norma said it was old and out of style when she gave it to me, but that it would be fine for me to wear to work at the restaurant."

Jennifer oohed and aahed as dress after dress was revealed and laid across the tables. She kept up a running commentary, punctuated with questions for Irma.

With only one box left to open, I said, "But we only have six mannequins." I wish I'd realized the treasure trove of fashion history that Irma had kept so many years.

"I'm wearing this one." Irma opened the last box and held up a classic Chanel suit.

"No way!" Jennifer said.

"Yes, way," Irma grinned. "And it still fits. Why don't you wear one of the dresses?" she asked Jennifer.

"Oh no, I couldn't." She looked both shocked and honored at the thought. "I'll be working, and I wouldn't want to take the chance of anything happening to it."

"Suit yourself." Irma glanced at me. "I'd offer one for you to wear, but—"

"I'll be working too," I said, before she could tell me I'd never fit into any of them.

"Where are the jewels?" Irma asked. "We need to pair them with the dresses. That might help us decide which ones to display."

"True," I said, "but I've been instructed not to take them out of the safe until the security guard arrives." The insurance company had given me strict instructions about when and how I could display them. "He's supposed to be here at five. That will give us two hours to arrange them before guests begin arriving." The invitation stated the event would start at seven, but I knew most attendees wouldn't make an appearance until seven-thirty or eight.

Jennifer spun around slowly, taking in the room. "What's left to do, then?"

I reviewed my to-do list one more time before answering. "I've got more appetizers to assemble, but I'm starving. Let's eat lunch!"

WHEN THE SECURITY GUARD ARRIVED, he followed me and supervised as I removed Norma's jewelry from the safe and put in the flash drive for safe keeping. I'd forgotten how dazzling the jewels were, as I examined the emerald and diamond necklace I'd last seen over a month ago.

I let Irma and Jennifer decide on the ideal necklace to pair with each dress, until Jennifer picked up the bug broach.

"No," Irma said. "You are not pinning that hideous thing on any of my gowns."

Jennifer scrunched up her face. "There must be a way to display it without poking holes in them." She inspected each dress, but the only way to attach the beetle was by the thick pin on the back.

"I have an idea," I said, hoping to make everyone happy. "Why don't you wear it, Jennifer?"

You'd think I'd told her she won the lottery by the grin she wore. "Really? But I'm wearing a tuxedo."

Irma nodded vigorously, happy to see the brooch as far as possible from her vintage dresses. "That's a great idea. It will look great with your tux."

I went back in the kitchen and took the blinis out of the freezer, popping them into the oven for a few minutes. I'd waited as long as I could to finish preparing them, afraid they'd get soggy. Once they were thawed I let them cool to room temperature and carefully scooped a dollop of creme fraiche on each little pancake, then followed up with a half teaspoon of caviar. I sprinkled finely chopped chives on the top.

"Wow," a woman's voice said. "Looks fancy."

I turned to see the Fiend, or rather the Friend of the Library I'd met weeks ago. "We're charging a lot for these tickets. I thought I should give them their money's worth. I don't think we've ever been formally introduced. I'm April."

"I'm Harriet." She proceeded to tell me everything about herself, where she grew up, what she'd had for breakfast that day, and more. I continued preparing the rest of the blinis as she told me about the paint chips she'd gotten from the hardware store so she could repaint her bedroom walls. "They're a hideous green right now," she said. "I'm thinking of a nice eggshell. Did you redecorate the tearoom yourself?"

"Huh?" I realized it was my turn to talk. "Oh, Jennifer took care of most of that. She's much more artistic than me. I do get veto power."

I covered the blinis and placed them carefully into the refrigerator, pulling out the jug of cold butterfly pea flower tea I'd made.

"I wonder how many of the guests will want champagne cocktails?" I mused. "Would you like to taste-test one?"

"What's in them?" Harriet asked.

While I prepared one for her to try, I explained they were a version of a French 75, with tea, simple syrup, and fresh lemon juice.

I handed her a flute with the purple drink. "I donated all the food and incidentals for the fundraiser, and Sebastian very generously donated two cases of champagne. We also have red and white wine for the less adventurous."

As if on cue, Sebastian entered the room, causing me to forget what I'd been saying. He could give James Bond a run for his money in his tuxedo.

Harriet's mouth dropped open while he greeted me with a kiss, then pressed her lips together tightly when I introduced her. She scurried away, as if frightened.

"Thanks for scaring her off," I said. "She was about to give me repainting tips, I think."

He grinned. "I came early to see if I could help with any last-minute tasks."

Jennifer appeared in the doorway, looking adorable in her tuxedo, her hair in braids, the bug brooch pinned to her lapel. "Don't you need to change?"

I gasped, looking down at my yoga pants. "I almost forgot." I turned to Sebastian. "I'll be as quick as I can."

"Take your time," Sebastian called after me as I hurried up the back stairs. "And try to relax."

Relax? Fat chance of that.

CHAPTER 19

I came down the stairs slowly, trying my best to walk gracefully in my high heels, and stopped on the landing to survey the room. The buffet stretched from the fireplace to the wall by the kitchen, already set up with everything that didn't need refrigeration. At the bottom of the stairs, opposite from the buffet, a makeshift bar had been set up. I'd pour wine and champagne cocktails for the first part of the evening, while Jennifer served appetizers. Then Jennifer would take over from me so I could assist Sebastian in his emcee duties.

The front of the room held several tables, with chairs arranged in rows facing the podium and the bay window. I walked down the remaining steps and over to the windows, releasing the sage-green velvet curtains from their tiebacks. They made a perfect backdrop for the speaker. I turned when I heard Sebastian's voice.

"I remember that dress from our first dance," he said. "I think it's about time for a reprise, don't you?" He took me in his arms and began swaying me back and forth, humming a tune.

I laid my head on his shoulder, feeling his jacket against my cheek, the scent of his cologne transporting me back to the first night we met.

He spoke softly in my ear. "I'll never forget the moment I first saw you."

I looked into his warm, brown eyes. "And I'll never forget how you rescued me that night." I laughed, enjoying the moment and letting the rest of the world disappear for a few moments. "My knight in shining armor, saving me from dull dance partners."

The doorbell rang, and he took a step back, holding both my hands in his. "I guess it's showtime."

Irma arrived first, looking chic in her Chanel suit, followed by Harriet in a tuxedo. "Harriet volunteered to help serve," Irma said.

I thanked Harriet and led her to the bar and showed her how to mix the tea and champagne cocktails along with the non-alcoholic versions. Luckily, I'd kept the options simple.

The next hour flew by as guests arrived. Irma introduced me to the members of the library council, who graciously thanked me for arranging the fundraiser.

A plump woman with shoulder length brown hair introduced herself as Rhonda Rafferty. "I'm so glad you're opening a tearoom." She pushed a pair of thick glasses up her nose. "I love tea."

"Me too," I said with a grin, realizing how lame that probably sounded. Would anyone open a tearoom who didn't?

"What will your hours be?" she asked.

"Starting tomorrow, noon until five every day but Monday."

A hint of disappointment showed as her smile slipped. "Well, I suppose that will have to do." She wandered off to get a drink.

Something about her name tickled a memory. The sisters

in the tragic story I'd read were Roberta and Cheryl Robinson. Cheryl had fallen from the lighthouse, but what about her sister? Was Roberta Robinson from Kyla's book really Rhonda Rafferty?

I pulled Irma aside. "Did Rhonda have a sister who died tragically?"

Her eyes widened in surprise. "How did you…" Understanding dawned on her face. "Did Kyla write about her sister's fall from the lighthouse?"

"She did. Was it really—"

I didn't get a chance to ask my question before I was interrupted by Harriet, who asked for more tea and lemon for the drinks. My special cocktails had turned out to be a big hit. Jennifer roamed the room with an appetizer tray held high, while Irma described the dresses on display to the guests. I repeated the story of finding the jewelry in my house until I thought I might lose my voice.

At eight, Sebastian asked if he should start the formal part of the festivities, and I eagerly agreed.

I stepped up to the podium. "May I have your attention, ladies and gentlemen." Several guests found seats and I waited for them to settle down. I thanked them for coming and for supporting the reopening of the library. "And now, I'd like to introduce someone most of you know, someone who holds a special place in his heart for the Serenity Cove Library. Sebastian Bernini."

"Thank you, Ms. May," he said, giving me a wink and waiting for the applause to die down before addressing the group.

He looked so handsome, captivating the room with his commanding presence and strong voice. He acknowledged the donors who had helped make the evening possible, giving me a special mention as I hid in the back of the room by the kitchen door.

As he talked about the library and what it meant for our little community, the front door eased open, and a small man slipped inside. I recognized the cowboy hat and bushy mustache—it was the same man who'd talked to Kyla at my party. He slipped around the crowd toward the buffet, where he ignored the food, instead keeping his eyes on Sebastian as he introduced Harriet.

Harriet droned on for ten or fifteen long minutes, reiterating the importance of the library to the town, until Sebastian gently coaxed her to turn the mic back to him. Next, he introduced Irma, explaining that she'd loaned the designer dresses on display.

Irma surprised me by giving a passionate speech about the meaning of community and how the library was the heart of Serenity Cove. When she ended, the audience responded with a rousing round of applause.

I glanced at the buffet to check on the cowboy, but he wasn't there, or anywhere that I could see. Had he left while Irma had held my attention? If he had, he must have slipped out the back door.

All thoughts of the cowboy left my mind when Mayor Wanda Gasden burst in. She stepped up to the podium and pushed the speaker aside, an elderly neighbor who'd lived in town her whole life.

"You people are anti-progress," the mayor bellowed. "Hardback books and paperbacks are a thing of the past."

Sebastian stepped up to her. "Mayor," he said, his voice firm but steady, "this isn't the time or place."

She continued, unswayed. "Converting the library building into a multi-use facility will bring jobs and tax dollars to the town." For emphasis, she pounded the podium as she spoke.

Irma stood up from the back of the audience. "If you knew what you were doing, we'd have plenty of tax dollars.

And everyone in town who wants to work already has a job."

"There will be a food court on the main floor, with gourmet options," the mayor announced to the crowd. "That's why she doesn't want the renovations to happen. She's just worried about her restaurant losing business. She only cares about herself!"

"That's enough." Sebastian grabbed her arm and pulled her away from the podium.

"Let go of me," Mayor Gasden bellowed, wrenching her arm away from him.

A man in the front row leapt up and snapped a picture of the altercation. The mayor stared at him, wide-eyed, then hurried for the door. I watched as she practically ran down the street.

Jennifer appeared next to me. "That should make a good headline in tomorrow's paper."

I sighed. "Why can't I ever get a nice article on page three about my lovely tearoom?"

WHEN THE LAST of the guests left, and Norma's jewelry had been returned to the safe, I carried the remaining glasses into the kitchen. I found Jennifer filling the dishwasher.

"Start that up, and let's leave the rest of these until tomorrow," I suggested. "I'm beat, and if you keep working, I'll feel guilty and have to keep working, too."

"I did want to meet up with some of my friends, if that's all right with you."

"Of course, but you don't have to ask me when you want to go out. You're a grown woman, and I'm not your mother."

Her eyes widened for just a moment, then she gave me a

shy smile. "You would have made a great mom." She hugged me then left the room.

A familiar voice said, "She's right, you know."

Chef leaned against the counter, his hands in his pockets as if he'd been there watching us. It must be tedious watching mortals talk and work, coming and going, while all you could do was observe them.

I pulled a stool up to the island. "I missed out on having kids, but now I feel like I have a daughter." I grinned. "And I didn't have to change diapers or deal with her during her teenage years."

He smiled, but there was a hint of sadness in it. "You missed out on children, but you don't have to miss out on love. You're an attractive woman. I'm sure there are plenty of men who would be interested in marrying you."

"Marrying?" I heard the surprise in my own voice. "I'm not sure I want to get married."

He raised his eyebrows and tilted his head as if he didn't understand what I'd just said. "I thought every woman wanted to marry."

I shook my head. "Maybe back in the fifties, when women had so few choices. Most women weren't as lucky as Norma to come from money. It gave her independence."

"And yet she eventually married," he said.

"Not until after you left." I didn't say the words "disappeared" or "died." No one knew what happened back then. I wasn't sure even Chef knew, and I didn't want to bring up a painful memory. Someday I would ask him what happened so long ago, but not tonight.

"Whether you marry or not, you deserve love." He took a few steps closer until I could see his silver-blue eyes and dark eyelashes. I'd never stood this close to him before. He reached out a hand and touched mine. I expected his hand to go right through mine, but it didn't. My skin tingled, a feeling that continued after he pulled away.

With all Emile had been through, he was still a hopeless romantic. Maybe I could be one too, or better yet, a hopeful romantic.

"Forgive me, but I spent many years in love with a woman who didn't return my affections. I have no desire to go through that again." He walked away from me, pausing as if giving me one last look. "Perhaps I've been a lovely dream you had. You imagined a chef who would keep you company in your kitchen so you wouldn't be so lonely. I'd like you to remember me that way."

I watched his image slowly fade away, trying to understand the meaning behind his words. "I'll never believe you were just a dream."

I stared at the spot where I'd last seen Emile, not wanting to tear my eyes away. I repeated his words in my head. Was that his way of saying goodbye?

A noise overhead distracted me from thoughts of my ghost chef. Whisk!

"Oh no! I forgot to feed him." I grabbed the bag of kibble and headed for the stairs. "I'm coming, Whisk."

I ran up the stairs and rushed down the hall to the attic door. As I reached out a hand to open it, something hit me on the back of my head, hard.

CHAPTER 20

I opened my eyes and tried to focus on the man staring at me anxiously.

"She opened her eyes," he said.

A woman's voice responded. "Thank goodness."

The voices sounded familiar. I turned my head to see who the other voice belonged to and groaned. Instinctively, I touched the back of my head. "Ow."

"Don't move." Jennifer's face appeared in front of me. "I called the paramedics. And Doc Severs. And the police."

"Where am I?" I lay on a hard surface, and the wallpaper and sconces told me I was on the floor of the upstairs hallway. I felt an icepack and pillow under my head and a blanket over me. "What happened?"

Sebastian spoke. "I came back to see if you needed help with the clean up and saw someone running out the back door. I found you out cold." He paused. "What do you remember?"

"I was talking to Emile," I said.

Sebastian took my hand. "Who?"

I heard the front door open and close but decided not to

move my head for the time being. Footsteps came up the stairs and headed our way.

"Chef Emile, you know..." I struggled to remember. Something about a dream, but I couldn't fit the pieces together. "The ghost."

"Wow." Freddie's voice sounded worried. "That must have been quite a blow."

Sebastian stood to get out of her way as Freddie opened her medical bag and proceeded to examine me.

"Is she going to be okay?" Sebastian asked, the concern in his voice evident.

"Good thing you got that ice pack on her, but she's going to have quite a bump." She shone a light in both my eyes, took my pulse, and checked my blood pressure. "She's okay to be moved. Do you think you can stand?"

"I'll carry her," Sebastian said, and I felt his strong arms scoop me up. He didn't even grunt or groan.

Jennifer led him to my room where he placed me gently on my bed.

"Who's this Chef Emile?" Sebastian asked, a note of jealousy in his voice.

Jennifer glanced at my nightstand where one of Emile's cookbooks lay. She handed it to Sebastian. "I think this is who she's talking about. She's obsessed with his recipes."

Sebastian flipped open the book. "This was published in 1960." He turned it over to look at the back of the faded dust jacket. "Not a bad looking guy. I suppose he'd be at least a hundred years old if he were still alive."

I reached for the cookbook and gazed at the picture of the handsome chef. "Such a lovely dream."

~

THE NEXT MORNING, Jennifer made me a cappuccino and filled me in on what happened after I went to bed. "Deputy Molina thinks it must have been a thief who attacked you."

I tentatively touched the back of my head. "Ow." I'd avoid doing that again for a while. "What makes him think it was a thief?" My thoughts went to the jewels. "The safe!"

"The safe wasn't touched as far as he could tell, but the upstairs parlor is a mess."

I climbed the stairs, and when I reached the parlor door, my heart sank. My desk drawers had been thrown open and papers and office supplies were strewn over the floor. *My laptop!*

I hurried to my bedroom and found the computer safely tucked away in my nightstand drawer. Thank goodness I'd put it there to keep it safe during the party. That's where it would stay from now on. I closed the bedroom door and locked it.

I took the steps back to the first floor, my mind full of questions and theories. The intruder must have been looking for Kyla's manuscript. But only Irma and Freddie knew I had it. Was the intruder the same person who'd killed Kyla?

I stepped into the kitchen, finding Jennifer making another espresso drink. "I hope that's for me. Whose idea was it to open for business the day after our grand opening?"

She spoke over the hissing cappuccino machine. "Um, yours?"

"Oh, right." At least we had all morning to get ready. The wonderful thing about a tearoom was the limited hours. "Better make that a double."

"Maybe we shouldn't open today," Jennifer said as she frothed a carafe of milk. "Freddie said you really should rest. We only have one reservation. Why don't I call and cancel?"

"I'm fine." I ignored the low-grade headache that had been

with me since I woke up that morning. "I'm excited to finally be officially open."

A FEW MINUTES BEFORE NOON, I went to unlock the front door and found a brown-haired woman waiting on the porch.

"Finally," she said.

"Hello." I stood back to let her enter. "Rhonda, isn't it?" I hoped I'd remembered her name correctly from the night before. Before I could ask anything else, she found a seat in the front corner on the opposite side of the room against the wall.

I watched in amusement as she settled in, then brought her a menu.

She waved away the menu. "I'd like a pot of your strongest black tea. That's all."

"That would be our English Breakfast tea blend. It's a mix of Assam, Ceylon, and Kenyan black tea."

"That will do fine." She moved the teacup and saucer in front of her as if impatient for me to fill it. "Milk and sugar please."

"I'll get that for you right away."

When I returned to her table with the pot of tea, I found her reading a book. I asked if she would care for scones or tea sandwiches.

"This will do just fine," she answered curtly.

The group who had made the reservations turned out to be a dozen members of the Tea-Totalers, a group for mature women who enjoyed afternoon tea. They livened the tearoom's atmosphere the moment they arrived with their enthusiasm.

After welcoming them to SereniTea, I seated them at

three tables, and handed out menus. One woman in a huge floppy hat and caftan appeared to be in charge. She handed me back the menu, declaring the SereniTea afternoon tea for all twelve along with three bottles of champagne, one for each table.

"We're T-E-A totalers," she explained. "Not T-E-E totalers."

After the ladies chose the types of tea they wanted, Jennifer and I got busy brewing several pots and opening the bottles. I picked up a tray of flutes, then leaned on the counter when a lightheaded feeling came over me.

Jennifer ran to my side. "Are you okay?"

"I'm fine." I gave her a sheepish grin. "Just give me a moment."

"Sit down. I'll take this out to the ladies." She picked up the tray and headed for the tearoom, calling back over her shoulder. "And you stay put until I get back."

One of the women said to Jennifer, "You seem under-staffed."

I called out from the kitchen. "She won't let me help."

Jennifer returned shortly for the champagne bottles. "Why don't you go to your room and lie down. I can handle them on my own."

The floppy-hatted woman appeared in the doorway. She chuckled. "Funny how you grow up and start telling your mother what to do, isn't it, dear?"

Jennifer glanced at me and smiled, but didn't correct the woman. "She was hit over the head last night by an intruder. She should be lying down."

"I feel fine," I protested, and moved to stand up.

"You stay put," the woman told me, then turned to Jennifer. "Bring out the champagne and we'll pour it ourselves. You've got quite enough to do."

"Thank you," I said with genuine gratitude.

From my stool at the island, I arranged the tiered trays full of sandwiches, scones, and sweets for Jennifer to place on each table. Floppy Hat then insisted that I join her at her table.

Before I took a seat with the ladies, I stopped at Rhonda's table to check on her. "Can I get you anything else?"

She looked up from her book and shook her head. "Is it always this noisy in here?" she asked, gesturing to the Tea-Totalers.

"It's our first day," I said, getting a shrug in response before she returned to her reading.

I spent the rest of the hour chatting with the ladies. Jennifer ran back and forth to the kitchen for hot water to refill the teapots, along with second helpings of scones and clotted cream.

Some of the ladies had been members of the Tea-Totalers since it first formed a decade earlier. It turned out that afternoon tea was one of their tamer activities.

"When I retired," another of the women said, "I decided that growing old gracefully didn't sound like any fun at all." Her friends heartily agreed.

"I went sky diving for the first time last year," a plump, pink-haired woman announced.

"You wouldn't catch me jumping out of a plane," I said. "The craziest thing I've ever done was buying this house and opening a tearoom."

The sky diving daredevil took my hand and gave it a gentle squeeze. "That sounds like a very brave thing to do."

"And more dangerous than one might think," Floppy Hat said to the others. "She had an intruder last night who hit her over the head."

Cries of "No!" and "Oh, my!" surrounded me, and someone asked, "Did it have something to do with the murder?"

"Murder?" someone else asked. "Someone was murdered?"

"You must have heard about it," Floppy Hat said. "That TV reporter. What was her name?"

"Kyla Bradley," I said, my mood instantly deflating.

"Did you know her?" the skydiver asked.

I nodded and blinked back a tear. "She was a friend. I didn't know her long, but I'm sad she's gone."

"Life is short," Floppy Hat said. "And it comes with no guarantees. You might as well make the best of what time you have."

CHAPTER 21

*W*hen Jennifer carried the last empty tray into the kitchen, I stood up to help her with the dishes.

"You sit back down," she ordered. "Freddie is stopping by in a little bit to check on you. Do you want me to fix you something to eat?"

"Are there any cucumber sandwiches left?" They'd been my favorite since I was a child.

"Coming right up."

By the time I finished the last sandwich, Freddie arrived. She gave me a quick check but couldn't find anything physically wrong.

She put her stethoscope away. "If you have any more symptoms of lightheadedness or weakness, let me know right away. I'll want to run more tests."

"I'm fine," I said. "I want to get back to figuring out who murdered Kyla. They're probably the same person that attacked me. Jennifer, grab me a notebook and we can make a list of suspects."

"I agree," Freddie said. "But not this evening. You're going to go to bed early and get some rest. And I don't want you working tomorrow either."

Jennifer piped up. "We're closed tomorrow anyway."

"But—" I began to protest but stopped when I saw the look in Freddie's eyes. I knew she had my best interests in mind, but I wanted to get started right away. "I'll rest better once I know who broke into my house."

Freddie folded her arms over her chest. "Irma and I will come over tomorrow, and we can talk then." She picked up her medical bag and turned to leave.

"I bet it's that cowboy," I blurted out before she reached the door. "We need to find out who he is and where he came from. He might be hiding a secret."

Freddie gave me a stern glare. "Tomorrow. Now go rest."

"As soon as I make myself a cup of tea," I said. As soon as Freddie left, I asked Jennifer for the notebook. I opened it and wrote Daniele and Cowboy on the page. That would have to do for starters.

I went upstairs, intending to climb into bed with a good book and read for a while at least until I unwound enough to fall asleep. I went into the upstairs parlor where a bookcase held several favorites and a few books I hadn't gotten around to reading yet.

I grabbed a popular novel I'd been meaning to read for years and took it back to my room. Glancing at my night-stand, I felt my laptop tempting me from inside the drawer. Maybe I shouldn't have copied Kyla's files onto my computer when I'd put the flash drive in the safe, but since I had, what could it hurt to read a little further?

I returned to an earlier chapter that I'd skipped over after a quick scan hadn't revealed any familiar details. Kyla had written *Year 2000* as a subheading.

The new century dawned, and once the residents realized that Y2K would not mean the end of civilization, life went on much the same as it had for decades. Fathers went to work, mothers kept house and volunteered in the community, and their children went to school and played on the sidewalks.

Many of those children grew up into entitled, demanding teenagers and young adults. Some went off to college, while others began careers in family businesses.

One young woman returned from college without a degree, having wasted her parents' money on two years of carousing and debauchery. Susan's father passed away in her absence, and her mother decided, perhaps later than she should have, that her daughter needed a firm hand and discipline.

Here the story went on for several paragraphs describing the misadventures of the young woman, who left town for a while, but always came back for more money. When her mother cut off her allowance, she was forced to move home. The fights between mother and daughter became more frequent.

I skimmed until the story became more interesting.

One night, after the neighbors reported hearing a particularly acrimonious argument, Susan stormed out of the house. When she returned the next morning, she found her mother dead from an apparent heart attack. She was heard to blame herself, saying "If I hadn't upset her, she might still be alive." Neighbors consoled her, secretly agreeing that the verbal altercation must have triggered the heart attack.

Susan was at fault, but not due to upsetting her mother. She had administered a lethal dosage of ethylene glycol, commonly used in antifreeze, by adding it into her evening drink. In the absence of evidence pointing to foul play, the death was ruled natural causes. Susan got away with murder.

The story went on to say that "Susan" had gone on to have a lucrative career, funded by her inheritance, and was considered to be one of the town's success stories.

I closed the manuscript file and stared at the blank

screen. As far as I knew, the only local woman who'd become a big success was Daniele Dubois, the soap opera star.

I searched the internet for information about her and her career, along with her family background. Her parents divorced when she was a child, and in the settlement, her mother got the Serenity Cove house where she continued to raise Daniele, whose real name was Sonia.

Susan. Sonia. In all the other stories, Kyla used the first letter of the actual name for the made-up name. I grinned. Not the sort of clue that could get Daniele convicted of murder, but it was a start.

THE NEXT MORNING, I bounced out of bed at dawn, my head full of suspects and clues. I threw on sweatpants and sneakers and headed down the stairs. After leaving a note for Jennifer so she wouldn't worry, I headed for the walking path along the beach. I had a lot to think about.

A gray mist hung in the air, and I pulled my sweatshirt closer around me to protect me from the chilly wind. Seagulls squawked overhead, the only sound other than the crashing waves. I took the concrete steps down to the beach, where the rhythmic waves nearly hypnotized me. Whenever I stared out into the ocean, the real world and all its troubles and cares seemed to melt away.

Not ready to let go of that feeling and return to the real world, I walked all the way to the lighthouse at the north end of the beach. The whitewashed structure stood at the top of the cliff, tall and lonely. Once lit by a five-wick oil lamp, it now aided navigation with an automated LED beacon. Not as romantic, but certainly more efficient.

The balcony surrounded the tower just below the lantern room, a black metal railing protecting anyone who stood there, but not Rhonda's sister. Why would any woman choose to end her life in such a dramatic way? Had it been her choice? Without witnesses, the truth might never come out.

I longed to climb to the top, but questioned if my motive was morbid curiosity. The idea that someone could be that despondent to even consider such an act tore at my heart.

For the past several years, the lighthouse had remained closed to the public, waiting for funding to restore the structure and make it safe to explore. Just another victim of the city's budget shortfall, or was that just an excuse to keep curiosity seekers away?

The sun crept higher in the sky, so I headed back, hoping that Freddie would stop by before she started her workday. As I approached my home, a convertible pulled into the driveway. I felt excitement at seeing Sebastian and then remembered the sweats I wore. I watched him walk up the steps to the porch and decided to sneak around the back.

He stepped back from the door just as I passed the side of the porch.

"April?"

I gave him a sheepish grin and headed toward him. "Oh, hi," I said, as if I'd just noticed him. "What are you doing here?" That might sound rude, so I added, "Nice to see you."

"I wanted to see you in person to make sure you were okay."

I unlocked the door and he followed me inside. "If you'll give me a moment, I'll take a quick shower and make myself look presentable."

"You look beautiful," he said.

"I didn't know you had vision problems," I joked and headed for the stairs. "I guess nobody's perfect, huh?"

When I came back down, I found Sebastian and Jennifer in the kitchen chatting.

"You two better not be talking about me," I said.

"Kinda." Jennifer jumped off her stool and headed for the espresso machine. "We were talking about the person who attacked you after the party. Do you think they were after something?"

I froze. Neither of them knew about the flash drive, or did they? "Like what?"

Sebastian spoke over the sound of Jennifer frothing milk. "Like the jewels."

"Oh, of course." I relaxed. "They're kept in the safe, and I'm the only one with the combination."

"Maybe it was a safecracker who hit you," Jennifer said. "Maybe he knows how to open safes without a combination, only Sebastian showed up, so he had to leave before he got a chance to try."

"Maybe." I gave her an indulgent smile. That wouldn't explain why they'd searched my upstairs parlor and made such a mess.

"Is there anything else valuable you keep in the house?" Sebastian asked. "Or important? Maybe something having to do with Kyla?"

"Like what?" Jennifer asked.

Sebastian looked at me as if I might have the answer. "I have no idea," he said.

The doorbell interrupted us, and Jennifer hurried to answer the door. Moments later, Mark appeared in the kitchen doorway. He glanced at Sebastian before turning back to me. His face appeared impassive, without his usual friendly smile. "Can I talk to you?"

"Sure? What's up?"

"Alone?"

He followed me into the front room where we took a seat by the bay window. If we spoke softly, we wouldn't be heard from the kitchen.

"I'm worried about you," he said.

"Really? Thanks, but I'm fine." I shrugged, as if getting attacked in my home was a regular occurrence. "It was just a bump on the head."

"I'm worried about you being in this house alone, just you and Jennifer." He glanced toward the kitchen. "I think we should install security cameras."

"I don't think that's necessary." When I arrived in Serenity Cove, I'd just sold my share of the business I'd started with my fiancé. That allowed me to buy the house and start the tearoom, but it would be a while before I'd turn a profit. I needed to watch expenses like any savvy business owner.

He leaned back in his chair and folded his arms. "If there were cameras, we'd know who attacked you the other night."

"Assuming they didn't have a sweatshirt pulled up or a ski mask. If you ask me, cameras only catch amateurs."

"How do you know your intruder was a pro?" He paused, but only got a shrug from me in response. "Will you at least think about it?"

"Okay, sure." I waited for him to get up, but he didn't move. "Is there something else?"

Mark leaned forward. "How well do you know Sebastian?"

"Sebastian?" I wondered what he was getting at. "Well enough. Why?"

"I don't trust him."

CHAPTER 22

*J*examined Mark's expression, trying to understand his reason for his words. "You don't trust Sebastian?"

He stood. "Just be careful, okay?"

"Okay." I walked him to the door. "Thanks for worrying about me."

I reached my arm out for a hug, and he wrapped his arms around me, holding me tightly for several seconds. He let go then left without another word. I watched him walk toward his truck, not sure what to think. Did he feel bad that the security system that he'd installed hadn't protected me? That was my fault for not arming the system the moment the last guest left.

When I returned to the kitchen, Jennifer let me know she'd be gone most of the day. "So you two can have some alone time," she said with a knowing smile.

I took a seat next to Sebastian at the island.

Sebastian reached out and took my hand in his. "I think he's jealous of me."

For some reason, the image of Chef Emile Toussaint

came into my mind. Funny how dreams can stick with you long after you've awakened. "Who?"

He laughed. "Your handyman."

I smiled. "He's just a friend."

"Good. I don't want to have to fight over you." He stood and smiled, the corners of his eyes crinkling. "Now that I know you're okay, I've got some business to take care of. Can I take you to dinner on Friday?"

"I'd like that." I walked him to the front door, and he gave me a brief hug. I couldn't help comparing it to the way Mark held me, as if he didn't want to let me go.

I watched Sebastian walk to his car. He was handsome, successful, and treated me well. What else could I possibly want in a man?

When I returned to the kitchen, I found Irma sitting at the island.

"When did you get here?" I asked.

"Just now." She scanned the room as if hoping to find baked goods. "I didn't want to interrupt you love birds. Seems like things are moving right along. Funny, I thought you and Mark would have ended up together."

"Why do you say that?" Not comfortable with the discussion, I went to the cupboard where I kept a few leftover muffins. I unwrapped them and put them on plates. I placed one in front of her along with the butter dish and a knife.

She touched it tentatively. "It'd be better warm, don't you think?"

I sighed, but she had a point. Getting up, I popped one in the microwave for a few seconds, placed it in front of her, and returned to my seat across from her.

"Is that better?" I asked, adding, "Your Majesty."

She regarded me intently. "You never noticed the sparks when you and Mark are in the same room?"

I shrugged, disappointed the muffins hadn't distracted

her from the subject of my handyman. I'd felt something but hadn't noticed any reciprocation, at least not until Sebastian entered my life. "Any woman who isn't half dead would have a reaction to Mark."

She grinned. "Good point."

There was a knock on the back door, and Irma called out, "Come in," before I got a chance.

Freddie was all business. "I've only got half an hour. Let's get to work." She took a seat at the island.

I stood to heat up a muffin for her, guessing she might not have had time for breakfast.

"Nice to see you too," Irma groused.

Freddie narrowed her eyes at Irma. "We need to find out who killed Kyla before April's the next victim."

I gasped and nearly dropped her muffin. "You think my attacker meant to kill me?"

"Until I know otherwise, that's what I'm going to assume. Do you have another explanation?"

I gave it some thought before answering. "Maybe he wanted the flash drive with Kyla's manuscript."

"Or she," Irma added. "It's in the safe, right?"

"Right." I popped Freddie's muffin in the microwave. They didn't need to know about the copy on my laptop. "I read another story last night." I summarized the story about "Susan" who, in the story, had murdered her mother. "She's supposed to be someone successful who grew up in town."

"Daniele Dubois?" Irma asked, swallowing the last bite of her muffin.

"That's what I was thinking," I agreed. "I did some research, and her mother died when Daniele was in her twenties. Is there any way to find out if she really had a heart attack?"

"Not sure," Freddie said, "but I'll see if her files are in our records. My dad was the county coroner back then and the only doctor for twenty miles, so he most likely was called on to sign the death certificate."

"Okay, so she's one suspect," I said. "And then there's the cowboy."

"The cowboy?" Freddie asked. "The one that was at your grand opening?"

"He was at April's party, too," Irma said, eyeing the muffin I'd placed in front of Freddie.

"That's right," I said. "And I saw him talking to Kyla. He whispered something in her ear."

TUESDAY MORNING, Jennifer and I prepared for the day ahead. Without any reservations for afternoon tea, we had no guarantee that we'd get a single customer, but we had to be ready just the same.

"We need to come up with some ideas about how to drum up more business." While we talked, I mashed hard boiled eggs for egg salad sandwiches. "Otherwise, we'll have to eat all the leftover egg salad and cucumber sandwiches."

Jennifer grinned. "I'm okay with that." She sliced cucumbers, putting them into a plastic container full of water. They'd keep fresh that way for several days in the refrigerator.

"You say that now." A sliver of worry hid in the back of my brain. I knew business would start off slowly, but I hadn't prepared myself for the day-to-day ups and downs. On any given day, we might have twenty guests. Or none.

"When summer gets here, you'll wish we had a slow day," she said. "Not to mention bridal showers and stuff like that."

"That may be, but summer business won't be enough for the tearoom to survive through the rest of the year. In the meantime, I've been thinking about special events. Something fun to bring people in and get some publicity." I added mayonnaise to the eggs, along with a dash of Dijon mustard. I preferred mine with dill and chives, but not everyone liked those ingredients, so I left them out.

"Ooh!" Jennifer practically bounced with excitement. "How about a My Fair Lady event?" She put her hands on her hips and did her best Eliza Doolittle impression. "'Allo, guvnor. 'Ow's about a cuppa?"

I laughed at her cockney accent. "Or Mary Poppins!" I tried my hand at a posh British voice. "Would you like a spoonful of sugar with your tea?"

We went back and forth for several minutes, throwing out idea after idea, from animal themes to Victorian teas.

"Ooh! We could have a Downton Abbey event. I have some Victorian reproduction dresses," Jennifer said. "We could both dress up in them."

"You used to dress up all the time." I scooped the egg salad into another plastic container and sealed it. "Is there a reason you stopped?"

She stared off for a moment as if a memory had intruded in her thoughts. After a long sigh, she said, "Maybe it's time to grow up. You know, be a responsible adult and quit playing dress-up."

"No!" I said, louder than I'd meant to. I softened my voice as I repeated, "No, no, no. Number one, growing up is highly overrated. Number two, never stop being who you are because of what you think others expect of you. Number three, the only reason to stop wearing your outfits is if it stops being fun. You need to jealously guard the fun that you find in life. Don't take it for granted, or you'll end up old and bitter like a dried-up prune."

Jennifer blinked a few times, apparently not sure how to respond.

"I mean, that's just my opinion," I added with a grin. "Sometimes I get a little carried away."

"I like that about you. And you're right." The smile returned to her face. "I love dressing up. Why should I worry what anyone thinks?"

"You work at a tearoom, Jennifer." I grabbed the egg salad and sliced cucumbers to put them in the refrigerator. "Everyone is going to love your outfits."

"I think I'll start today. I just got a new psychedelic dress from the thrift store in Hiverton, and I have the perfect go-go boots to pair with it. I'll try it on so you can see what you think."

She practically skipped up the stairs, returning minutes later in a hot pink and orange paisley minidress and white boots. "What do you think?" she asked shyly.

"I love it." A thought popped into my head. "Princess Di."

Jennifer raised her eyebrows. "No. This outfit is from the sixties. I don't think she was even born yet."

"She was born in 1961, but that's not what I meant. We can have an event to celebrate her birthday on July first." I checked the calendar hanging on the kitchen wall. "That's a Thursday. We can have a weekend celebration." Disappointed at the lack of response from Jennifer, I asked, "You don't like the idea?"

"I suppose that could be, um, nice."

"Nice? I'm going to go on social media and find all the fan groups. It will be an awesome way to kick off the summer!"

Jennifer didn't appear convinced. "If you say so."

A few minutes before noon, I went into the tearoom to unlock the front door and found Rhonda waiting again. She nodded a hello then took her place at the same table she'd sat at on Sunday.

When I entered the kitchen to make Rhonda's pot of tea, I told Jennifer, "It looks like we have our first regular."

She poked her head into the room to see who I meant. "That's nice, I suppose. At least she's low maintenance."

I cringed and quickly looked for wood to knock on. "I hope you're right."

As it turned out, we had six more customers for the day—a mother and daughter, and four middle-aged women who had been friends since college. I learned that they got together every year and had been doing so since they'd graduated.

"I'm so glad you opened the tearoom," one said. "We used to go to San Francisco to one of the hotels, but this is much more intimate. And your scones are fabulous." Her friends agreed enthusiastically.

"Spread the word," I told them. "And you don't have to wait until next year to come back."

Rhonda left before the others. "See you tomorrow," she called out as she left.

Yep. Our first regular.

After closing, Jennifer and I dined on tea sandwiches. We'd no doubt get tired of them eventually, but I'd been craving cucumber sandwiches since watching her prepare them that morning.

As the evening progressed, I began to feel restless. We'd made almost no progress figuring out who'd killed Kyla or who'd attacked me on the night of my grand opening. Did we have one person in Serenity Cove with murderous intent? Or two?

CHAPTER 23

I let Jennifer know I'd be going out for the evening. "I thought I'd stop by the Mermaid Cafe and see Irma." I wanted to see if she'd given any thought to my theories or the identity of the cowboy. "Would you like to come along?"

She shook her head. "Thanks, but I think I'll stay home and read."

"Okay, but keep the doors locked. I'll arm the security system, so remember to turn it off if you go outside. Better yet, don't go outside."

She gave me her best eye roll. "I'll be fine."

The weather had begun to warm up, but as soon as the sun dipped below the horizon, the temperature would drop twenty degrees. Not sure how late I'd be, I grabbed a jacket and crossed the street to the path that led along the ocean to the pier and Irma's restaurant. The sun touched the water, ready to make its descent. As I walked, stripes of clouds turned from cotton candy pink to magenta and purple.

Walking past the pier, I breathed shallowly, hoping to

keep the fishy smell out of my nostrils. The last of the anglers packed up their gear and prepared to leave.

Opening the door of the Mermaid Cafe, I stepped into the fanciful, sea-themed interior. The contrast from the shabby exterior never failed to surprise, and the magical feeling that came over me each time I entered had not yet faded. I hoped it never would.

I found a spot at the bar with the more colorful patrons. A young, handsome bartender took my order and poured me a glass of white wine. I sipped it while waiting for Irma to notice me. I watched her in her mermaid outfit complete with multicolored wig as she flitted from table to table.

The restaurant served delicious food at a fair price, but I firmly believed that most diners came to see Irma. Apparently, her no-nonsense approach and wicked humor appealed to many of the locals, though I had no doubt she'd offended many others who probably stayed away. I felt sure that was just fine with her.

I'd just taken out my phone to make some notes and organize my thoughts, when her voice startled me.

"I was beginning to think you'd forgotten the way here," she said, in her usual sarcastic tone.

"I've been a bit busy." Talk about an understatement.

"How much did you raise for the library?" she asked. "Enough to reopen it?"

"I think so. My accountant is crunching all the numbers. Then the Friends of the Library can apply for the matching grant." I gave her a sly grin. "Maybe there'll even be enough for them to order new T-shirts."

She chuckled. "I certainly hope not. I rather enjoy calling them Fiends." Her eyes caught someone over my shoulder. "Hi, Doc."

I swiveled in my seat to greet Freddie. "Hey, fancy meeting you here."

"Jennifer told me where to find you." She lowered her voice. "Have you made any progress on tracking down the cowboy?"

"None." I waited impatiently as Irma went to the other end of the bar to deliver a drink.

"I've been giving it some thought," Irma said when she returned. "Have either of you ever seen Daniele Dubois in person?"

"Not me," I said. "I only saw her on that dancing show. She looks good for her age."

"I have," Freddie said, "but it was years ago. I'm not sure I'd recognize her. I don't watch much TV."

"Do you remember how tall she was?" Irma asked.

Freddie gave the question some thought. "Around my height, I think. Five foot six or so, I'd say."

Irma turned to me. "How tall would you say the cowboy was?"

"I suppose he was about..." I realized what she was getting at. "That mustache! I should have realized it was fake."

"What are you two talking about?" Freddie asked.

"They're the same person," I said. "The cowboy is Daniele Dubois."

CHAPTER 24

*W*ednesday morning, I checked the reservations just to make sure no one had magically booked during the night.

I checked our supplies to make sure we had enough food in case we got some drop-in customers. I'd made a mix for the scones so that all I needed to do was mix in heavy cream, then roll them out and bake them. If I had extra dough today, I planned to freeze some unbaked scones and see how they came out.

"You'd think the segment WSTV did on the grand opening would have brought in more people for afternoon tea," Jennifer said.

"Kyla would have done a much better job on the segment. She was such a talented reporter." I stopped pacing and plopped on a stool. "And a good friend. I wish I had told her when I had the chance."

My phone buzzed with a message from Freddie about Daniele's mother's death. Although it appeared to be natural causes, they hadn't performed a tox screen to rule out poison. She ended the message with, *I'll stop by tonight if you're around.*

Next, I reached Deputy Molina on his cell phone, and he agreed to see me. Ten minutes later, I sat in front of Molina's desk explaining that we'd figured out that Daniele Dubois and the mystery cowboy were one and the same.

"What does that tell us?" he asked. "Going around in disguise doesn't make you a murderer. Maybe she just didn't want to be hounded for autographs."

"No, but there's a story—" I stopped myself.

"Go on," he prompted. When I didn't respond, he added, "You were about to tell me that you have a copy of Kyla's manuscript, I believe."

I slumped in my chair. "Fine. I have it. But most of the stories are totally made up. If you read it, you'd think Irma and Freddie had motives for murder, but they don't. Kyla exaggerated everything to make it more dramatic, perhaps hoping to sell more books that way. The truth is usually pretty boring. But she wrote about Daniele."

"She used her name?"

"No, of course not. She wrote about a woman whose mother died from natural causes, but Kyla claimed it was murder."

Molina made a few marks on a notepad on his desk. "And you think it's about Daniele because...?"

"Because the person she wrote about went on to be very successful. And Kyla used the same first initial for her fictional counterparts. She called the character in her book Susan and Daniele's real name is Sonia."

"I can't arrest someone because Kyla put their initial in a book," Molina said. "Besides, you said yourself that most of the stories aren't even true. What makes you think this one is?"

"I saw the cowboy, who we now think was Daniele,

talking to Kyla the night she died. She could have easily put the poison in the drink. And Freddie says there's no way to know if Daniele's mother actually died of natural causes since they didn't do any tests to see if she'd been poisoned. There was no reason at the time to suspect foul play."

He leaned back in his chair and folded his arms. "Dr. Severs doesn't believe the poison was in Kyla's drink."

I blinked, trying to make sense of his words. "Drink, food, whatever. What's the difference?"

"The difference is, Dr. Severs doesn't believe the toxin was administered at your party. Based on Kyla's symptoms and time of death, she estimates she was poisoned earlier that afternoon."

I stared at him, feeling my confidence fade. "That means anyone could have killed her. We've been limiting our suspects to people at the party." I slumped in my seat. "Oh, man, now what?"

"Now you leave it to me," he said. "And maybe now you'll hand over the manuscript."

"Fine," I said, "but you may regret it."

"Because of all the clues and details I'll have to sift through?"

I grimaced, not wanting to speak ill of the dead. "Because the writing is terrible."

WE OPENED the tearoom at noon as usual. Rhonda took her regular spot, and we waited for more customers to arrive. And waited. Finally, a family of three—a woman with her mother and young daughter arrived mid-afternoon. Jennifer served while I baked scones and made sandwiches. I froze the remaining unbaked scones to bake later. Tomorrow, we'd have a taste test to see if Jennifer could tell the difference.

Irma would likely stop by as well, and she was always perfectly happy to try anything I baked.

While I busied myself making grilled cheese sandwiches and heating up soup for Jennifer and me, Freddie stopped by. I offered to make her a sandwich, but she had dinner plans.

"Why didn't you tell me you found out Kyla wasn't poisoned at my party?" I asked, annoyed that she'd kept that information from me.

She gave me a smirk. "What do you think I'm doing here right now? I just came to that conclusion this morning."

"Oh, sorry." I gave her a contrite smile. "That changes things, doesn't it? Here we were trying to narrow down the suspect list, and now it's just been widened. I still think Daniele killed her to make sure no one would find out that she killed her mother."

"Except she didn't." Freddie must have seen my confused look, because she went on to explain that Daniele was out of the country when her mother died.

"Then what is she doing in town in disguise?" I asked.

"I have an idea about that," Jennifer said. "When I was little, Daniele was a big star. She'd get mobbed everywhere she went, so a lot of the time, she'd wear a disguise."

Freddie nodded. "Now, if she went out without a disguise, she'd probably be ignored. She might consider that worse than getting mobbed."

I sighed, then noticed the soup boiling over. I turned down the heat and gave it one last stir. "I guess it's back to square one."

BEFORE GIVING the flash drive to Deputy Molina, I felt the need to take one more look at Kyla's manuscript to make sure I hadn't missed any incriminating information. Especially now that our best suspect had been scratched off the list.

I pulled my laptop from the nightstand drawer and leaned back against the pillows. I opened the file and read the next chapter.

The Smiths appeared to be a happy family from the outside. Mr. and Mrs. Smith attended the local church, and their daughter Jessica grew up loved and well cared for.

Kyla had to have been writing about Jennifer. I hesitated, not sure if I should read on. Kyla made up some terrible lies and exaggerations about my other friends, and I began to wonder what kind of person she really was. It seemed unnecessarily cruel.

Still, I wanted to know what else she had written. If Jennifer or her family had a secret, I wanted her to be prepared.

The cracks in the veneer began to appear when Jessica went off to college. Mrs. Smith told her husband she was leaving him. They planned to wait until Jessica finished her freshman year, but Mr. Smith made life unbearable for his wife.

Jessica came home for a visit and could feel the tension between them. Her mother confided that she was leaving her father but feared he would become violent. She hatched a plan to drive Jennifer back to her school and keep driving to another town where she would start a new life.

Mrs. Smith left that day with only the clothes on her back and a few thousand dollars in cash. With her daughter driving the car, she thought her nightmare was over.

That night, on a dark road, her daughter lost control of the car and swerved into a tree. Jessica called her father—her mother was unconscious. He told her to switch places with her mother so she wouldn't be charged with involuntary manslaughter, and he would be on his way. Jessica panicked and did as she was told.

No one may ever know for sure if moving Mrs. Smith or the

delay in calling the paramedics contributed, but when Jessica and her mother arrived at the hospital, Mrs. Smith was declared dead. Jessica eventually recovered, but was left to live with the consequences of her actions.

I stared at the screen. No wonder Jennifer hated anyone bringing up the accident. I shook my head to dislodge the idea. Everything else Kyla had written had turned out to be lies. What made me think this story was any different?

Still, I'd promised to give Molina the flash drive with Kyla's manuscript, and if he saw what I'd just read, he might decide it warranted investigation. At the very least, it would bring up terrible memories for Jennifer, and I didn't want to do that to her.

I turned off the laptop, closed it, and slipped it back into the nightstand drawer. I'd decide what to do in the morning.

CHAPTER 25

J sat at the island with my coffee while Jennifer looked through the cupboards, deciding what to eat for breakfast. She finally chose cereal, and I waited as she picked out a bowl, poured the cereal, and added milk. She took a seat across from me at the island.

She must have felt my attention, because she pulled her eyebrows together in a worried expression. "What?"

I hesitated, but I didn't see what other choice I had. "I need to ask you about the accident."

Her spoon stopped halfway to her mouth as she stared at me wide-eyed. She put it back in the bowl. "Why?"

I swallowed, not really wanting to go on. "Kyla wrote about it. I have the manuscript."

"You do? Why didn't you say anything?"

"The fewer people who knew, the better. Especially you, since you live here. I didn't want to put you in any kind of danger."

She waited for me to go on, a hint of suspicion in her gaze. I hoped I imagined it.

"I've read most of her manuscript. Most of what she

155

wrote was fabricated, but based loosely enough on the truth that it seemed believable. I'm sure that's the case with what she wrote about you and your family too." I paused, but she didn't make a sound, so I went on. "Kyla wrote that you were driving the car and you moved your mother into the driver's seat so you wouldn't get blamed for the accident."

It broke my heart to see the hurt in her eyes before she broke eye contact. I hated causing her pain. I waited for her to say something, but she stayed silent, staring at her bowl of cereal.

"I promised Molina I'd give him the flash drive, but I wanted you to know what was on it first." Still no response from her. "Why don't you tell me what really happened, and I can tell him, so he'll know it's all a lie."

Jennifer broke out in sobs and ran out of the kitchen. Her footsteps pounded as she ran up to her bedroom room and slammed her door.

I felt my heart twist in my chest. "I would have made a terrible mother," I mumbled to myself. Now what was I supposed to do? I did the only thing I could think of—I sent a text to Irma and Freddie. *I screwed up. Need help.*

Within minutes, Irma's three raps sounded at the back door. I opened it and after taking one look at me, she threw her arms around my waist. I stood awkwardly holding my breath as she held me tightly.

"Is that enough?" she asked.

"Enough." I let the air out of my lungs as she let go.

"Good. I hate hugs. What's going on?"

"Kyla wrote about Jennifer." I summarized for her, telling her what the story claimed Jennifer had done during and after the accident that claimed her mother's life. "Now she's shut herself up in her room."

"We'll see about that." Irma headed for the stairs. I called out after her, and she returned, her hands on her hips. "What?"

"I think she needs to be alone, at least for a little while," I said.

"And what does Freddie have to say about all this?"

I showed her the text I'd sent and her reply. *Busy. Talk later.*

Irma scowled. "How dare she have a life. Does she really think her patients are more important than we are?"

"Some people," I said, glad to have my friend with me. Irma could lighten any situation, at least a little bit.

Irma seemed to understand that I needed company, so she stayed while I prepared to open the tearoom. I set a pot of water on the stove to boil more eggs while I peeled and cut up cucumbers. Meanwhile, Irma ate about half the cucumbers I sliced, but I didn't mind.

Shortly before time to open, Freddie burst through the back door. "I don't have much time, so pay attention."

I nodded and listened as she shared what she'd learned.

"Jennifer's mother's injuries were consistent with her being behind the wheel."

"So, Jennifer *wasn't* driving?" I asked.

"Not only that, but Jennifer was unconscious when the ambulance arrived." She paused, and in a quiet voice added, "Her mother was already dead."

"Then why did Kyla—?" I began. "Wait. Never mind what the book says. Why does Jennifer think that she was behind the wheel if she wasn't?"

Freddie shook her head. "I read the report. Her father arrived at the scene of the crime just before the paramedics did."

"I remember when it happened," Irma said. "Rumors had circulated that Jennifer's mother had decided to leave her husband. I usually don't give much credence to rumors, but I think they were true in this case. You know he lost his mother when he was a child, and now he found himself losing his wife."

"Maybe he was afraid of losing Jennifer too," I said. When the others gave me strange looks, I explained my thoughts. "What if her father made up the story so she'd feel guilty and wouldn't leave?"

Irma's mouth dropped open. "But that's horrible."

"He'd scarred his daughter for life, but perhaps in his mind it was better than losing her forever."

Freddie shook her head sadly. "I've heard about worse parenting than that, believe it or not." She stood to leave. "I'll be back later tonight if I can."

Irma and I sat at the island nibbling on cucumbers, each of us lost in our thoughts.

After several minutes, Irma said, "Now can I go up to her room?"

"I think it should be me." I had to tell her that she wasn't responsible for her mother's death while at the same time exposing her father's betrayal. "I hope she takes it okay."

I stood in front of her door getting my courage up. When I knocked, she didn't answer. The second time, she called out, "Go away." Then, "Leave me alone."

I stood outside the door and told her what we'd learned. "We love you and we're here for you, whatever happens." She didn't answer, but I heard her sobs from the other side of the door.

THE NEXT MORNING, I sat in the kitchen alone with my instant coffee. Molina sent me a text letting me know he'd be by that evening to pick up the flash drive.

I let Rhonda in ten minutes before opening. I figured as

our only regular customer she deserved special treatment. I tried to make conversation with her, but her one-word answers told me she preferred to be left alone.

Besides her, the day's tearoom customers included two sisters who chatted nonstop through their afternoon tea. They were paying their bill when a middle-aged couple arrived. I could tell the husband clearly didn't want to be there.

I never understood why so many women loved everything about afternoon tea, while so many men didn't. Hoping to win him over, I suggested the plowman's lunch, complete with cold meats, cheese, bread and pickles. The wife gave me a grateful look, and they appeared to enjoy the rest of their meal. He left with a full stomach and a smile on his face.

Jennifer hadn't come out of her room, only sending me a text asking for the day off. I brought her a tray of sandwiches, yelling through her door that she could have as much time as she needed but she needed to eat.

I retrieved the notebook where we'd written our suspect list. I reluctantly crossed off Daniele's name, leaving only the cowboy. I added Mr. Skillings' name. Would he have killed Kyla to keep the secret that he'd lied to his daughter? Jennifer had been through so much, I prayed he wasn't guilty of murder.

The kettle began to boil, and I made a pot of peppermint tea, hoping it would help me to relax and focus. I carried my cup to the fireplace and found a comfortable spot on the sofa. After staring at the ashes for a while, I threw on a log and turned on the propane to light it. It might be June, but a chill stayed in the air.

I'd been promised a warm and sunny July, but I'd wait and see. I'd put up with another month of gloomy weather if it meant no one else got murdered.

I'd just gotten comfortable with my stockinged feet

stretched out to take advantage of the warmth of the fire when the doorbell rang. I turned to see Deputy Molina looking in. I'd forgotten he planned to stop by.

With everything that had happened, I'd become much better about keeping all the doors and windows locked, which meant I had to get up to let him in.

"Have a seat," I said, motioning to the wingback chair. "I'll get you the flash drive and a cup of tea."

When I returned with his tea, I found him gazing at the crackling fire. "You sure have a nice house. You know, outside of the murder and people breaking in."

"Yeah, they left that part out of the brochure," I joked.

He gave me a quizzical look, then chuckled.

I handed him the flash drive and told him what we'd learned about Jennifer. "Freddie confirmed that part of the story is a lie. She wasn't driving that night."

He took a sip of tea. "That's not half bad."

"Thanks. I used to drink black tea all day, but the caffeine kept me up at night, so I'm trying some herbal blends. I find peppermint invigorating without the insomnia side effect." I picked up my cup and savored the minty aroma. "So now we know that pretty much everything in Kyla's manuscript was fabrications, exaggerations, or outright lies. I'm starting to doubt that's what got her killed."

He nodded. "The problem is, I haven't uncovered any other possible motives." He put his cup down and stood to go. "I guess I'll be doing some reading tonight."

"You might want a cup of strong coffee to help keep you awake."

I CARRIED a cup of kibble up to the attic for Whisk. Did he ever get lonely up there with no one around? I often left the door ajar in case he wanted to join us in the rest of the house. As far as the health department was concerned, it was probably best that he stayed where he was.

"Hey, Whisk," I called out. "I brought you dinner."

I filled his bowl and took a seat in his favorite Windsor chair. I didn't blame him for hanging out up here in his own personal hideaway. No one to bother him. No murders to solve.

Molina hadn't made any more progress on the investigation than I had. Once I'd learned that Kyla had been given the dose of toxin before she even arrived at my party, I had to admit that we might never find out who murdered her.

Anger filled me at the thought that someone might get away with murder. I couldn't let that happen. I didn't know what I was going to do about it, but I'd think of something. I had to.

I felt something rub against my leg and reached down to pet Whisk. He jumped up in my lap and kneaded my thighs like he was about to bake a fresh loaf of bread.

"I might have to put you to work," I said. "I never got the hang of kneading bread."

He circled my lap then curled up and fell asleep, his loud purrs vibrating pleasantly. A warm cat on your lap was surprisingly comforting. I leaned back in the chair and closed my eyes.

When I awoke, the attic, shrouded in darkness, felt otherworldly, as if a ghost might appear at any time. I chuckled at the thought. "There are no such things as ghosts, April. You know that."

Whisk was nowhere to be found, so I made my way carefully to the stairs. I climbed down to the second floor, then turned the hall light on and continued the rest of the way. As usual, I ended up in the kitchen.

I felt a desire to be comforted, to feel like everything

would be okay. I considered making another pot of tea, but when I opened the cupboard, a bottle of cream sherry caught my eye. After pouring myself a glass, I found a bar of dark chocolate and took them both to my favorite spot by the fireplace.

The log had burned down to an ashy glow, so I added another which quickly caught fire. I listened to it snap and pop while I sipped my drink. The chocolate, creamy and rich, melted on my tongue.

I hadn't seen Sebastian since Monday. That was only three days ago, so it surprised me to realize that I missed his company. When summer was over, he'd go back to the city full time. Would he bother to make the two-hour drive to come see me then? I would enjoy seeing him from time to time, but it wasn't the same as having someone to talk to every day, cooking side by side, bantering and bickering. A memory tugged at my brain of a handsome French chef. Just a dream. I sighed. Why did I miss something that wasn't even real?

I went to take another sip of sherry, surprised to find the glass empty. Another glass couldn't hurt.

CHAPTER 26

The moment I opened my eyes the next morning, I groaned. How much sherry had I drunk the night before? Enough to give me a nasty headache, but not enough to take my mind of Kyla's murder.

I sent a text to Irma and Freddie. *I must have missed a clue in the ms.* I dreaded reading Kyla's entire manuscript again, but if that was what it took to find a killer, I would. If my friends would agree to help, we could split up the task.

Irma was the first to arrive. When I let her in, she huffed at me, though I didn't know if she was annoyed about the text or because the back door had been locked. I locked it behind her.

She pulled up a stool and plucked a muffin from the platter in the center of the island. "I thought you gave the flash drive to Deputy Molina." She broke open the muffin. "Where's the butter?"

I handed her the butter dish. "I kept a copy on my laptop," I admitted. "I'm convinced I'm missing something. Maybe I'm grasping at straws, but what else do we have to go on?"

Irma lowered her voice. "You don't think Jennifer's father killed Kyla, then?"

I put my chin in one hand, my elbow on the island. "I don't want to think it, but we've run out of other suspects."

"He didn't kill Kyla." Jennifer's voice startled me, and my heart dropped into my stomach. How much had she heard?

"Of course, he didn't," Irma said. "He would never do such a thing."

Jennifer walked over to the cupboard and grabbed cups and saucers. She scowled at the jar of instant coffee on the counter. "Are you really drinking that stuff?"

I shrugged. "You're going to have to teach me to use that darned machine one of these days."

Another knock on the door meant Freddie had arrived, and Jennifer let her in, offering to make her an espresso drink.

Jennifer had a question for the doctor. "You think Kyla had been poisoned before she ever got to the party, right?"

"I'm quite sure of it," she said.

Jennifer nodded as if reassuring herself. "I had to know for myself. I had to know if my dad was a..." she swallowed, "a murderer."

The three of us waited in the uncomfortable silence, giving her time to share what she needed to say.

Jennifer took a deep breath and exhaled. "I went to the antique store last night after you went to bed. He doesn't know I still have a key." She gave me a sheepish smile. "I checked the security tapes. We, that is he, has cameras covering the front and back entrances. I fast forwarded through them. He arrived at the shop a little before nine-thirty in the morning and didn't leave until after six."

"I estimate Kyla had been poisoned sometime between four-thirty and five-thirty that afternoon," Freddie said.

Jennifer smiled, the first real smile I'd seen from her in days. "So, you see, my dad couldn't have poisoned her."

I jumped off my stool and gave her a hug, whispering in her ear, "I'm so glad."

"That's great detective work," Irma complimented her. "Of course, I never thought your father could murder anyone."

"Of course not," Freddie added.

Jennifer insisted on making coffees for everyone, and I watched her flipping switches and foaming milk. I hated to think about all the pain she'd been through at such a young age. I wanted to do something to make it up for her, but what could I do?

Pancakes might not fix a broken heart, but they could be surprisingly comforting. I got out my mixing bowl and started cooking. I made enough for all four of us, and I could have sworn they put color back in Jennifer's cheeks.

While the others ate, I reviewed my suspect list. "I'm really happy that we've added to our list of people who did *not* murder Kyla." I didn't try to hide my sarcasm. "Can we try and make some progress on who might actually be guilty?"

"You think there's a clue in Kyla's book?" Irma stabbed another pancake from the stack and slid it onto her plate. "Let's have a look at it."

I went up to my room, returning with my laptop. After making sure I'd wiped up all the maple syrup, I set it up on the island and opened the manuscript file. "I'll summarize the stories for you guys."

I quickly went through the story about how "Ida" pushed Norma down the stairs. Next was the story about the doctor's death. I paused, not sure how to proceed, not wanting to bring up painful memories for Freddie.

Freddie saw my hesitation and filled in the blanks for the

others. "It basically says I killed my dad. Like a mercy killing. Which I didn't."

Irma shuddered. "Of course, you didn't." She scowled at me as if I'd been the one to accuse Freddie. "Go on."

I returned Irma's scowl and continued. "The next story is about a woman named 'Susan.' I couldn't figure out who it referred to at first, since Kyla used the real person's first initial in her made-up names. But then I found out that Daniele's real first name is Sonia."

I summarized the rest of "Susan's" story. Irma stopped me when I got to the part about her mother's death.

"Did you say that Susan in the story lost her father when she was a child?"

I sighed, not wanting to hear criticism of my latest theory. "I know. Daniele's father outlived her mother."

"And she didn't inherit anything from her parents until he died around ten or fifteen years ago," Irma said. "She was already a big star by that time."

I skimmed through the story again. "Kyla got lots of details wrong in all of the stories. I'm sure it made it less likely that she'd be sued. But that doesn't mean Daniele didn't murder Kyla. She was here in town that day."

"But what was her motive?" Freddie asked. "We know she didn't kill her mother. She wasn't even in the state at the time."

Another thought came to me. "Could she have killed her father?"

Freddie shook her head. "He died after a long illness."

Irma stared at the remains of buttery syrup on her plate, her thoughts somewhere else.

"What is it?" I asked. "Do you want more pancakes? You've already eaten about five." I stood up. "I can make more. Anyone else?"

Irma reached out to stop me, and her eyes met mine. "Sebastian's father died when he was a child."

"I know. He told me all about his parents." I didn't like where this conversation was going. I took our plates over to the sink, rinsed them off, and put them in the dishwasher.

Freddie spoke up. "He was in his early twenties when his mother died of an apparent heart attack." She gave me a solemn look. "Her body was cremated."

"But Susan is a woman," I protested, returning to my seat at the island. "The details are all wrong."

Freddie's eyebrows drew together. "But you just said Kyla liked to change details—"

"I know what I said." I stood up again, nearly knocking over my stool. "It can't be Sebastian." I walked over to the sink and stood with my back to them, not wanting to listen to another word.

Irma didn't get the hint. "Did you sleep with him?"

"What?" I spun around to face her. "No, of course not."

Irma lifted one shoulder. "I wouldn't have blamed you. That man is—"

"Would you stop it!" I didn't want to hear any more of their madness. Could the man I'd spent so much time with over the past two weeks really be a murderer?

I put my hands on my hips, wanting to appear more confident than I felt. "Then who hit me over the head? It couldn't have been Sebastian. He's the one who found me."

The three women fell silent while I vigorously sponged off the island.

Jennifer spoke first. "Did he?"

I looked from her to Irma. She nodded, as if confirming what I didn't want to believe.

Freddie sucked in a breath. "Think about it. He's on the second floor looking for the flash drive when you come up the stairs. He hits you over the head so he has more time to search or maybe escape. By the time you come to, he's come up with a story that he came back and saw someone leave out the back door."

I sat back down on the stool, leaned my elbows on the counter, and put my head in my hands.

"This is not happening."

CHAPTER 27

reddie called Deputy Molina, stepping outside to talk. I stood by the door, hoping to overhear her conversation, but she noticed me eavesdropping and closed it. *Rude.*

I returned to Jennifer and Irma, standing in the middle of the kitchen trying to decide what to do with myself.

"Another cappuccino?" Jennifer asked.

"I think I'll make a pot of strong Darjeeling tea." I put the kettle on and glanced at her. "Now we both know what it's like to have someone close to us accused of murder."

Irma scraped her stool as she stood. "At least you weren't a suspect yourself, the way you suspected me."

"I never thought for a moment you killed Kyla," I said, which was true.

"You just thought I pushed Norma down the stairs," she said.

"Not on purpose," I clarified. "She sounded like a piece of work. I might have given her a shove if I'd known her."

That got a smile out of Irma. "I'm the picture of restraint. All my attacks are purely verbal."

Freddie returned to the kitchen but didn't take a seat. "Deputy Molina said he'll go question Sebastian later today." She must have seen the look on my face, because she added, "Don't worry, I told him to make sure not to involve you."

That was easy for her to say, but I was involved. Despite my misgivings, I thanked her.

Freddie had patients to see, and Irma walked out with her. I imagined the two of them discussing how to prove Sebastian was a murderer.

"We don't open for a couple of hours," Jennifer said. "If it's okay with you, I'm going to go see my dad." She didn't appear happy about the idea. "I need to know the truth about what happened to my mom."

"Do you want me to come with you?" I wanted to help but had no idea how.

"No, I'll be fine." She gave me a hug and went upstairs to get her things. A few minutes later, I heard the front door close.

Now that I was alone, I could take another look at Kyla's book and find a clue leading to the real murderer.

I PUT a batch of scones in the oven, half fresh and half frozen from the day before. Taking a seat at the island, I stared at Kyla's manuscript on the laptop screen. If someone killed her because of one of the stories, they must not have known how little truth she'd written into her book.

My friends wanted me to consider Sebastian as a suspect, but they hadn't spent time with him. They hadn't heard the way he talked about his mother or seen his kindness and compassion the way I had.

Why would anyone kill Kyla over a rumor-filled bunch of exaggerations and mistruths? Just to stop her from publishing her novel? With so many overwrought, overly dramatic accounts, no single story would stand out. Sure, there would be a flurry of gossip as the rumors spread, but they'd soon die down and things would go back to normal.

I couldn't bring myself to read the stories again. I wanted to believe I'd missed a clue the first time around, but I began to lose hope. I'd done all I could. It was time to delete the files from my computer and let Deputy Molina handle the case from now on.

I opened the file folder I'd copied from Kyla's flash drive, and my eyes went to a zip file labeled 'recipes.' I was always on the look for new recipes, so I unzipped the file, but instead of recipes there were twenty or so pictures. I opened the first, a screenshot of a text exchange.

Kyla: *What proof do you have?*

Andrew: *Audio file.*

Kyla: *Proof Sebastian killed mother?*

Andrew: *Yes*

I stared at the screen. Kyla could have created fake text messages and taken a screen shot. Maybe she used them to blackmail Sebastian, but that didn't mean he killed her. I wondered how many other people she'd tried to blackmail.

Scanning the laptop screen, I found an audio. That might be the recording that held the supposed proof. Before I could open it and listen, I heard the front door open. I closed the laptop and stuffed it in the cabinet where I kept my cookie sheets. I'd have to remind Jennifer to keep the doors locked, even during the day, at least until my attacker was identified and put behind bars.

I closed the cabinet door just as Sebastian entered the kitchen. I let out the breath I'd been holding when I saw his warm smile. How could anyone believe him capable of murder?

"Hi!" I grinned back at him, relieved that he was here to reassure me. "What are you doing here?"

"Hey, beautiful." He stepped closer and wrapped me in a comforting hug. I closed my eyes, doing my best to push suspicion out of my mind.

The timer went off and I reluctantly pulled away, taking the scones out of the oven.

"I missed you," he said. "I hope you don't mind that I didn't call first."

"Of course not." I motioned to one of the stools. "Have a seat. I need a taste-tester for my scones. You have good timing."

I poured each of us a cup of tea and set a plate with two scones in front of him along with homemade clotted cream.

"Let me know if you can tell the difference. One of them is made from frozen dough." I tried to act naturally, but found myself unable to make eye contact. My thoughts kept returning to Kyla. Why did Irma and Freddie have to make me doubt myself? I had good instincts, and I could trust my feelings.

Sebastian took a bite of each scone, chewing thoughtfully. "I can't tell the difference at all."

"Great!" I said, possibly a bit too enthusiastically. I moved to the counter, transferring the remaining scones to a platter. I looked around for something else to do to keep busy and began emptying the dishwasher.

"April."

I stopped what I was doing. "Yes?"

He patted the seat of the stool next to him. "Come sit down."

I stepped over to the island, taking a seat across from him instead.

"Do you have something on your mind?" he asked.

Say no. I took a deep breath. "Why'd you stop back by the night of the open house?"

He lifted one eyebrow. "I told you. I wanted to see if you could use some help cleaning up." He reached over the island and took my hand in his, giving it a gentle squeeze.

That made sense. Or did it? "Then why did you leave in the first place?"

His eyes darkened and he pulled his hand away. "What's bothering you?"

"Nothing," I lied. I picked up one of the scones and slathered it with clotted cream before taking a bite. I chewed the suddenly tasteless, doughy mass, finally washing it down with a swallow of tea.

He seemed to be watching my every move. "You're not acting like yourself."

I tried and failed to suppress my nervous laughter. "I'm acting exactly like myself. Haven't you noticed that I ask a lot of questions? I've been told it's both my best and worst trait."

He smiled, but not the warm, kind smile I'd seen before. Had his charm and friendliness been an act so he could get close to me to find out what I knew? To find out if I had Kyla's manuscript? Or maybe it was the audio file he was after.

"What do you want to know?" He reached across the island, once again taking my hand in his. "I'm an open book."

Fighting the urge to pull my hand away, I ignored the voice in my head telling me to play it safe and say nothing. "You mentioned your father died when you were young, and your mother kept busy with her social duties. That must have been hard for you."

He pressed his lips together, as if holding the truth inside. "All she cared about was her standing in the community. She controlled her image and her reputation, and she wanted to control me." He stood and stepped away from the island, not

173

looking at me as he spoke. "When I left college, she cut off my allowance—said I couldn't be trusted with money. I had to ask for every dollar." He walked back to me, standing close, his face inches from mine. "Do you know how humiliating that is?"

I stared into his unblinking eyes, taking slow, even breaths in a fruitless effort to avoid panicking.

He broke eye contact and walked toward the counter where my knife rack sat, stroking the handle of my newly-sharpened carving knife "She even accused me of stealing from her purse. Can you imagine?"

I said nothing, too anxious to trust my voice.

"Then she cut me off completely. I had to do something, don't you understand?" He pulled the knife from the rack and smiled again, a smile that was more of a sneer. "Don't you?" He took a step closer to me, the knife hanging at his side.

My mouth dry, I tried to swallow. "What did you do, Sebastian?"

"Where is the flash drive?" He lowered his voice, and a chill ran down my spine. "I know Kyla gave it to you."

I shook my head, stalling. Should I tell him that Deputy Molina had it? What would he do to me then? He'd killed his mother, and he'd killed Kyla. I had no reason to think he wouldn't kill me. I knew too much.

"That was very clever putting the toxin in the pickles." I hoped a little flattery might make him less murderous, if only temporarily. "How did you manage that?"

He stroked the back of the knife and smiled again, proud of his plan. "I stopped by the mayor's office earlier that day. Pauline couldn't stop bragging about her pickles and told me all about you and your party. She even told me Kyla would be there. I'd already planned to take care of that scheming blackmailer but putting the botulinum in the pickle jars made it look like an accident. Or at least it should have. Still, it diverted attention from me until I could find out where she'd hidden the flash drive."

That part of his plan turned out to be less than perfect, but I decide not to mention that. "Then you met up with her before the party."

"I asked her to meet me at the hotel bar for a drink. I told her I just needed a few days to come up with the money, and she bought it. She said she'd give me the flash drive with all the evidence as soon as she got the money."

"But you killed her first. Did you slip the poison in her drink?"

"Enough questions." He raised the knife, pointing it at me. "Where's the flash drive, April? I want it now."

I needed to buy more time. My mind worked furiously to come up with a plan. "Upstairs."

He stood. "In your room?"

I shook my head and forced out the words. "In the attic."

Sebastian motioned for me to show him. I stood on shaky legs and led him up the rear staircase to the second floor. He followed me through the attic door. Whisk had saved me once, could he do it again? If he couldn't, I'd be stuck in the attic with a murderer and no way to escape.

I climbed the attic steps, feeling his breath on my neck as he stayed close behind me. The cat was nowhere to be seen. I stepped carefully between the boxes toward the window I always left open for Whisk to come in and out. Could I escape through that window? Not likely.

A memory flashed in my mind. A man's voice spoke from a dream. *Watch your step.* Then the words of another man came to me. Mark. *Watch out for the rotten floorboards.*

I stepped from one crossbeam to the next, hoping Sebastian wouldn't notice my careful footsteps. "Look out," I said, pushing a box aside, hoping to distract him from the floor beneath him.

The box tumbled and Sebastian cried out as his foot fell through the attic floor. He sunk in up to his thigh and dropped the knife. Before I could run back to the stairs and escape, he reached out and grabbed my foot.

"Give me the flash drive," he demanded, tightening his grip on my leg. "Give it to me now." With his other hand, he reached for the knife, which lay just out of reach.

I relaxed the leg he held, and he focused on reaching for the knife. With all the strength I could muster, I kicked, hitting him below the belt. He cried out, surprised enough to relax his grasp on me. I jerked my leg away and ran down the stairs, locking the attic door behind me.

As I rushed down to the main floor, I nearly ran into Deputy Molina. "Sebastian," I huffed. "In the attic." I struggled to catch my breath. "Murderer."

CHAPTER 28

I lay in bed, not bothering to get up or take a shower. Saturdays should have been our busiest days, but no one would want to come to my tearoom now. Last month a murder occurred on the premises and yesterday, a murderer was caught in my attic.

The land line rang incessantly. Reporters or nosy neighbors? I didn't care which it was. I wasn't answering.

Jennifer knocked on my door. "April? Are you coming downstairs? I'll make you a mocha double-shot latte."

"I'll be down soon." Maybe in an hour or two. What was the point?

"I really, really need you to come down." Her pleading tone must mean that she didn't want to handle all the phone calls herself.

When I finally entered the kitchen, Jennifer practically danced around the room, handing me my coffee drink and a pad of paper with a list of names and phone numbers.

"What's this?" I asked, doing my best to focus on the scribbled writing. The phone rang again, and Jennifer picked it up on the second ring.

"SereniTea Tearoom, how may I help you?" her melodic voice announced. "I'm sorry, but the earliest reservation I have is at four o'clock." She paused as the person on the other end of the line spoke. "Tomorrow? Let me see." She took the list back from me. "Yes, I can fit you in at two o'clock tomorrow afternoon. What's the name?"

I stared at her, dumbfounded. "We're booked?"

"Yes. Why do you think I've been trying to get you to come out of your room for the last hour? We'd better get going. We need to make around a thousand sandwiches and bake a ton of scones."

"But—"

"Don't worry," she gave me a comforting pat on my shoulder. "I took a limited number of bookings for this weekend. I think we should ease into handling a full house, don't you? But we've got bookings for every day next week and the following weekend too."

"But why?" I asked. "Why do so many people want to come here after everything that's happened?"

Jennifer's grin went from ear to ear. "Don't you know? You're a hero!"

I stared at her dumbfounded, not knowing how to take what she'd just said. "I don't feel like a hero." Besides, right now, I needed to get ready to open the tearoom.

I guzzled my mocha and threw on my apron. After quickly perusing the contents of the refrigerator and freezer, I made a shopping list and sent Jennifer to the store.

I hardly knew where to start. This was going to be fun!

THE LAST GUEST LEFT, and I collapsed into one of the chairs. Irma knocked on the back door and Jennifer told her where to find me.

"You look like crap," Irma said with a twinkle in her eye.

"Thanks." I brushed a lock of hair from my face, having given up on taming my ponytail. "That may be, but I survived."

"The kitchen looks like a war zone," she said. "Don't expect me to help clean up."

I gave her a half-hearted laugh. "I'm considering throwing all the dishes out and getting new ones. Or maybe I'll switch to paper plates."

She regarded me with concern. "I'm starting to worry. It's getting harder to offend you."

I waved a hand in dismissal and then let it fall to my side, so tired I could barely move. "Did you just come to gloat at all the work I have to do? We have to do this again tomorrow, you know."

"We applied for the matching grant." Irma looked pleased with herself. "The money raised from the fundraiser put us just over the amount needed."

"Now what?"

"Now we wait." She pointed over my shoulder. "Freddie's car just pulled into the driveway." Walking to the front door, she opened it and called out, "We're in here."

Freddie wore a tank top, shorts, and sandals. She flipped her sunglasses up on her head as she entered, greeting us cheerfully.

For the first time that day, I noticed the sun shining outside. I'd been too busy until now to even look outside. "Where's the June gloom?" I asked. "There's still five more days of June."

Before they closed the door, a voice called out my name. Harriet hurried toward us, wearing her bright orange Fiends of the Library shirt. How disappointing that they'd be able to order new ones now.

She burst through the door. "She's a traitor," she said, collapsing into a chair.

"Who's a traitor?" I asked.

"Pauline. She's at the library right now with the mayor. They put through a resolution at the city council meeting last night, and they're meeting with the architect right now."

"You must be confused," Irma said. "City council meetings are on the second Tuesday of the month, not on the fourth Friday."

Harriet shook her head. "This was a special meeting. They did everything by the book, but did their best to make sure as few people knew about it as possible. That's how they got it through. And Pauline didn't even warn us."

"That's it," I stood, anger giving me a second wind. "I'm going to the library and have it out with her." I grabbed my purse and keys, then remembered I was missing some important information. "Um, where's the library?"

"249 Elm Street," Irma said. "I'll go with you."

"Me, too." Freddie headed for the door.

"Who's driving?" Irma asked. "I call shotgun."

"Wait." That address sounded familiar, but why? Everyone stood impatiently while I probed my memory. When I retrieved the memory, I ran up to my desk upstairs, returning with the deed I'd found in the box in the attic. I'd read it in the car. "Let's go."

"I'll drive," Freddie said, and we all piled into her car.

Minutes later, we pulled up in front a white stucco building with red-tiled roof that appeared to be nearly as old as my home.

"What a charming library." I climbed out of the car and surveyed the scene. "I've seen homes in towns that look similar in style. What do you call the architecture? Spanish?"

"Mediterranean Revival," Harriet said. "Designed in the

late twenties, but not completed until 1930. The grounds were designed by…"

She kept talking while I walked up the wide stone steps to a pair of massive wooden doors. As I reached for the ornate bronze handle, the door swung open. It would have hit me if I hadn't taken a quick step back.

Mayor Wanda Gasden emerged, tall and sturdy as ever. She wore a red power pantsuit, the effect somewhat diminished by what looked like spit-up on her collar. As a new mother, perhaps she hadn't fully mastered the art of the burp cloth.

"You're too late," she announced, a triumphant smile on her lips. "The resolution has passed, and this building will reopen early next year as a multi-use space combining an upscale food court on the first floor and office space on the second." She spoke as if she were giving a press conference, and I glanced behind me to make sure reporters hadn't appeared.

"Mayor Gasden," I said, about to spring a surprise on her and my friends. "You might want to hold off on your gloating."

Her smile turned into a sneer. "You're too late, *April May*." She said my name as if it were a curse. "You're all too late."

"Not so fast." I did my best not to sound smug, but it wasn't easy. "I have a deed here for this property." I let that sink in before delivering my bombshell.

"Your deed means nothing," she huffed. "The city owns this property."

"You're absolutely right," I happily agreed. "But this deed contains a restriction dated 1928 stating that the land was donated to the city by Augustus Thornly on the condition that a library be built. It further states that no other use can be made of the property in perpetuity."

She took a step closer. "What are you talking about?"

"In perpetuity means forever," I explained.

Her eyes glowered. "I know what perpetuity means. Let me see that." She tried to snatch the document from me.

I clutched it tightly. "I'm happy to send your lawyers a copy." I didn't trust her and had no idea if I held the only copy of the deed.

She put her hands on her hips and puffed up her already sizable chest. "No one's going to enforce such an old restriction."

A man in a suit and hardhat appeared in the doorway, apparently having overheard our conversation. "Call me when or if you clear this up." He walked down the stairs toward a white truck parked on the street.

"Wait," the mayor called out, chasing after him. "Don't go!"

Harriet watched as the mayor ran down the sidewalk, then opened the library door. She stepped back, motioning for us to enter. "Let me show you around our beautiful library."

As I followed the others in, Harriet stopped me. "I almost forgot." She pulled something bright orange from her bag.

I unfolded a T-shirt that said, "Fiends of the Library."

Irma reached out her hand to shake mine. "Congratulations. We all voted to make you an honorary member."

"Thanks," I said without enthusiasm. "With friends like all of you…" I began. "Or should I say fiends?"

Irma gave me a nudge. "At least you'll never be bored."

CHAPTER 29

I returned to my kitchen, finding Jennifer and a smaller stack of dishes and cups than when I'd left. She looked relieved to see me.

"Sorry I left you with such a mess," I said. "Why don't you call it a night, and I'll finish up in here."

She brightened, wiping her hands on a dish towel. "A friend asked me to dinner. Unless you had plans…"

"Go," I said, waving her out the door. "Have fun."

Her mention of dinner reminded me I hadn't eaten since that morning. I checked the refrigerator for leftovers and found a container of French onion soup. As I heated it on the stove, the scent of the broth triggered a memory.

I could almost hear a man's voice with a French accent saying, "Did I not display the proper amount of enthusiasm?" I laughed.

"I miss you, Emile." How could I miss someone I'd never met? And why miss someone so overbearing and bossy? The dreams floated in my mind just out of reach—something about a hallucination. I'd called the doctor and drove all the way to San Francisco for an MRI.

183

Wait. I didn't dream that part. I really did go see the doctor. If that part was true, then what about the rest? But ghosts weren't real. Were they?

Goosebumps ran up my arms and my scalp tingled.

A voice, Emile's voice, said, "You may wish to attend to your soup before it boils over the top."

I spun around. There was Chef Emile Toussaint.

"You're back." I couldn't remember when I'd been so happy to see someone. "Where did you go?"

"I have told you, ma chérie," he said with a hint of a smile. "I am always here."

The End

~

Tea is for Tragedy
Book 3 in the Haunted Tearoom Cozy Mystery series
January 3, 2022.

Sign up for my (mostly) weekly email with updates, sales, freebies, and other fun stuff! (Not to mention stories about my rescue dog Kit including pictures).
https://karensuewalker.com

And read on for recipes!

RECIPES

PALMIERS

Yield: 20-24 cookies

INGREDIENTS:

- 1 sheet puff pastry, defrosted
- 1 cup granulated sugar (coarse-grained/raw sugar recommended to add a nice crunch, but regular is fine)

INSTRUCTIONS:

1. Lightly roll the dough to even out seams.
2. Sprinkle all but a tablespoon or so of the sugar in an **even** layer on the dough. With your rolling pin, press the sugar into the dough.
3. Lightly trace a line lengthwise (you can use the

back of a knife) down the center of your dough. (If your pastry is a square, just trace the line down the middle).

4. Fold each side in so they meet in the middle at your traced line, then fold in again.
5. Sprinkle with the reserved sugar and run rolling pin lightly over it.
6. Now fold one half over the other as if you're closing a book.
7. Refrigerate 30 minutes.
8. Heat oven to 425 degrees F.
9. Evenly slice into cookies about ¼ to ½ inch thick and place on parchment-lined cookie sheet.
10. Bake 6 minutes (they won't look done on the top). Turn and bake another 3-5 minutes until both sides are browned. Transfer to baking rack to cool.

April's note: This is such an easy dessert to make. You can add very finely chopped nuts and your favorite spices such as cardamom or cinnamon for a fun twist!

FRENCH ONION SOUP

Yield: 4 servings

INGREDIENTS:

- ½ cup unsalted butter
- 4 cups sliced yellow onions
- 32 ounces beef broth
- 3 Tablespoons Worcestershire sauce

- 2 Tablespoons dry sherry (can be omitted if necessary)
- Salt to taste
- 4 slices French bread, toasted
- 4 slices gruyere, swiss, or provolone cheese

INSTRUCTIONS:

1. Melt butter in Dutch oven or other large pot over medium heat.
2. Reduce heat to medium-low and add sliced onions. Sauté, stirring often, until blond in color, 20-30 minutes.
3. Add beef broth, Worcestershire, and sherry. Simmer for 10-15 minutes.
4. Just before serving, preheat broiler. Place oven-proof bowls, crocks, or soup mugs on a baking sheet and ladle soup into them.
5. Top each serving with a slice of toasted bread and a slice of cheese and place under broiler. Broil until cheese bubbles and browns slightly.

Chef Emile's note: Taking the time to properly caramelize your onions is the key to an acceptable result that will please the palate.

PAN FRIED SABLEFISH AND CANNELLINI BEANS

Yield: 2 servings

INGREDIENTS:

For the mash:

- 3 Tablespoons olive oil
- 1-2 garlic clove finely chopped
- 1 can cannellini beans, drained

For the sauce:

- ¼ cup olive oil
- ½ ounce basil leaves
- 1 teaspoon capers in brine, drained (optional)
- 1 garlic clove, peeled

For the fish:

- 2 Sablefish (black cod) fillets, about 6-8 ounces each
- 1 Tablespoon (or so) flour
- 2 Tablespoons olive oil
- Salt and pepper to taste

INSTRUCTIONS:

1. Prepare cannellini mash. Sauté garlic in oil over medium heat for one minute. Add beans and cook for 8-10 minutes, stirring occasionally. Season with salt and pepper and gently crush the beans

with a potato masher or fork. The beans should be lumpy.

2. Prepare basil sauce by pureeing basil, oil, capers, and garlic in food processor or blender. Set aside.

3. Heat olive oil in skillet or sauté pan over medium heat. Lightly flour fish filet and season with salt and pepper. Sautee fish skin side down for 3 minutes. turn and cook for 2 additional minutes.

4. Spoon cannellini mash on plate, place fish fillet on top, and drizzle with basil sauce.

BLINI WITH CAVIAR AND CRÈME FRAÎCHE

Yield: 40-50 blini

INGREDIENTS:

- ½ cup buckwheat flour
- 1 cups sifted all-purpose flour
- 2 teaspoon sugar
- ½ teaspoon salt
- ½ teaspoon baking powder
- ¼ teaspoon baking soda
- 2 cups buttermilk
- 2 Tablespoons unsalted butter, melted
- 2 large eggs, separated
- 1 Tablespoon vegetable oil plus additional for cooking blini
- Crème fraiche (or sour cream)
- 4 to 6 oz. chilled caviar (also wonderful with smoked salmon)

- Freshly sliced chives or minced shallots for garnish

INSTRUCTIONS:

1. In medium bowl, whisk first six dry ingredients.
2. In a separate bowl, mix buttermilk, melted butter, egg yolks (reserve whites), and oil. Add buttermilk mixture to dry ingredients and stir briefly until combined.
3. Beat egg whites until stiff and fold into batter until just combined.
4. Add small amount of vegetable oil to a large non-stick frying pan or griddle. Set over medium heat for about 5 minutes (or set electric griddle to 350 degrees F).
5. Use tablespoon to scoop batter into pan. Cook 3-5 at a time until bubbles appear on surface and begin to pop (about 2 minutes). Flip and cook until second side is light golden brown.
6. Serve blini with a dollop of crème fraiche or sour cream and top with chilled caviar or smoked salmon. Garnish with sliced chives, minced shallots, or chopped hard-boiled eggs.

SERENITEA PURPLE 75 COCKTAIL

Yield: one cocktail

INGREDIENTS

- ¼ cup butterfly pea flower tea, brewed strong
- 1 teaspoon lemon juice
- 1 teaspoon simple syrup
- ½ ounce gin or brandy (optional)
- Champagne, sparkling wine, or sparkling water

INSTRUCTIONS:

1. Pour all ingredients into a champagne flute, stir gently, and enjoy!
2. For the non-alcoholic version, add the lemon last to watch the color change from blue to purple.

Thank you for reading Tea is for Toxin,
a Haunted Tearoom Mystery!

∾

What's next for April May, Irma, Jennifer, Freddie, and Chef
Emile?

TEA IS FOR TRAGEDY

A Haunted Tearoom Cozy Mystery #3

April May is getting settled into her new home running her
little tearoom, when a stranger appears in town asking about
a death from decades earlier.

Will someone else die before April can solve the mystery?

For information about current and future books in the
Bridal Shop and Haunted Tearoom cozy mystery series, visit
my website at https://karensuewalker.com.